MW01257513

Books by Richard Helms

Geary's Year
Geary's Gold
The Valentine Profile
The Amadeus Legacy
Joker Poker
Voodoo That You Do
Juicy Watusi
Wet Debt
Paid In Spades
Bobby J.
Grass Sandal
Cordite Wine
The Daedalus Deception
The Unresolved Seventh
The Mojito Coast
Six Mile Creek
Thunder Moon
Older Than Goodbye

RICHARD HELMS

GRASS SANDAL

For Elaine

CYK!

ONE

Taylor Chu was dead.

It said so in the *San Francisco Chronicle*, on all the local radio stations, and on the six o'clock television news.

The death of Taylor Chu was a major story, given his renown as a courtroom defense attorney, and particularly due to the grisly nature of his demise.

Taylor had tossed a lot of business my way over the years. Without him around, I would see a significant hole in my cash flow.

I was sitting in my office, savoring the bottom half of my second jigger of Glenlivet single malt, and chucking darts at a baseball board propped at the far-right corner of my desk. I had scored five runs in the last two minutes. It was getting to be a bit of a rush.

My office was on the second floor of a small building on Jefferson at Fisherman's Wharf. Outside, sea lions were serenading a solid wall of fog as it rolled over Mount Tam and started to swallow the Golden Gate. Within minutes, I wouldn't be able to see Alcatraz, which was fine by me.

I was expecting visitors.

They arrived just as the fog settled enough to leave the towers of the bridge piers poking above the mire. There was an insistent knock at the door. Before I could answer two men walked in. The first, the obvious boss, was about my height, just a little over six feet, and his clothes smelled like the camphor balls his wife put in the closets to keep the moths away.

The gold badge on his jacket told me he was an Inspector First Class with the SFPD. The twisted scowl on his face told me he was here on business. Five years as my partner in a black and white bubbletop, cruising the tough streets of SoMa until a decade earlier, told me he didn't like it much.

"Gold," he said. It fell somewhere between a greeting and just the acknowledgement that I was in the room.

"Inspector."

I tried to ignore the other one. He was taller, and a damn sight dumber, and the few times I had crossed paths with him left me with the disappointingly cynical impression that he had benefited greatly from somebody's juice down at the Civic Center.

Frank Raymond, my former beat partner on the force, lowered himself into one of the leather-upholstered chairs facing my desk. His current partner, Dexter Spears, remained standing.

Frank stared at me. He always did that. I think he was counting his blessings that he hadn't gone down my path.

I picked up the bottle of Glenlivet and poured another half-jigger.

"Want a snort?" I asked.

Frank looked over his shoulder at Spears, and then back at me. His face looked tired and shopworn. Twenty years as a cop will do that to you.

"Did you really just use the word *snort*?" he asked.

"Comes with the territory. What can I do for you, Frank?"

As if on cue, Spears came to life.

"We have a problem," Spears said.

"Have you tried Viagra, Dexter?"

"Can you spare some, Gold?" he said.

"Oooh," I said, turning to Raymond. "Do that again, Frank. Then do the thing where you make him sing while you're drinking a glass of water."

Frank Raymond smiled briefly, but I noticed he was careful not to let Spears see it.

"Have you seen the news?" he asked.

I tapped a copy of the *Chronicle* on my desk. The headline read '*NOTED TRIAL ATTORNEY SLAIN*'.

"Yes, Frank, I have."

"Then you should know why we're here."

"I figured you would drop by sometime today."

"Want to tell us where you were over the last seventy-two hours?"

"No."

"Why's that?" Spears asked. He liked yanking my chain.

"Because then I would have to hire a sign painter to re-letter my office door," I said, pointing toward the frosted glass with the legend *EAMON GOLD, Discrete Investigations* on it.

"You need to do that anyway," he said. "*Discrete* is misspelled."

"Only for the linear thinker, Spears. Perhaps the average investigator would think the *e-e-t* version more appropriate. However, among its many meanings, the word *discrete* is a synonym for 'special, singular, or diverse'. You are right, though. It was intended to be *discreet*. You wouldn't believe the deal I got on the painter. If I tell you where I was the last several days, I would not be *discreet*. I do have other clients besides Taylor Chu. They pay me to keep our matters private."

"Cut the shit," Raymond said.

I took a sip of the single malt and smacked my lips. It was rude.

I didn't care.

Didn't have to.

"If you're asking whether I killed Taylor Chu, cut off his hands, feet, and head, and dropped him off the Bay Bridge, the answer is no."

"You can prove that?" Spears said.

"You're just going to have to take my word for it, unless you want to get a court order. You do that, though, and you are going to piss off some very powerful people."

"Your other clients..." Spears said.

"Among others."

Frank Raymond said, "We can hash all this out later. We came to you because you were working for Chu. We thought maybe you knew what he was working on, might have an idea who would want to toss him off the bridge."

"Move aside, Spears," I said.

"What?"

I sighed.

"Take your right foot, lift it off the ground, and put it down again, about one foot to your right. That's the hand you eat with. Then do the same thing with your left foot."

"We gotta put up with this asshole?" he asked Raymond.

"Just move aside," Frank told him.

Spears stepped to his right, and I tossed one of the darts between him and Raymond. It described a perfect arc as it traversed the office, before landing feathers-up in the top of the sealed banker's box I had prepared for just this moment and had placed by the door.

"That's what you want," I said. "All my records of my work for Taylor Chu. They aren't going to do me any good sitting around the office. He sure as shit isn't going to keep paying my retainer. I don't think he gives a damn about confidentiality anymore. Take it."

Spears started to cross the room to pick up the banker's box. Frank didn't move. He just stared at me.

It was kind of creepy.

"Sure you don't want a snort?" I asked.

He shook his head, sadly.

"You know, Eamon, someday someone is gonna cut off those big brass balls of yours and hang them in front of a pawn shop."

"My goodness, Frank, who told you I have three?"

"It's in the air. You could choke on all the testosterone in this room."

He rose from the chair and turned to Spears.

"Let's go. We still have a few stops to make."

He turned back to me.

"This is all of it, Eamon?"

"Every last scrap. I... uh, did keep some copies of specific items."

"And why did you do that?"

"Public relations," I said. "Someone flings one of your better customers off a bridge, it looks good if you check it out a little."

"I don't want you interfering with an active investigation."

"Hell, we both know who did this."

He paused for a second, glanced back at Spears, and then nodded as he turned back to me.

"Meaning?"

"Someone kills a guy, then lightens him by the weight of his hands, feet, and noggin, and tosses him into the Bay. Smells like gang shit to me. If I were you, I'd be sniffing down along Grant Avenue, check out the tongs. Do we think alike?"

"Yeah. Maybe we do. I'd appreciate it if you didn't get in my way, though."

"I'll keep an eye out for you," I said.

Without another word, Spears hefted the banker's box with Taylor Chu's records, and the two of them left the office. I could hear them clomping down the stairs to the street. After the outer door at the sidewalk slammed shut, I heard a toilet flush in the bathroom adjoining my office.

"You can come out now," I said.

The door opened, and the fellow who had been hiding in the bathroom walked out and sat in the same chair where Frank Raymond had been a minute earlier.

"I hope to hell," I said, "that this isn't some kind of sick joke."

"Me too," Taylor Chu said as he reached for the Glenlivet.

TWO

I have two houses. One I bought, and the other I inherited.

The house in town I bought with the insurance money I got after my first house, the one in the Marina District, was totaled in the '89 Loma Pieta quake. It managed to remain standing during the actual quake, only to be immolated when the gas furnace in the house next door blew up and took out half a block in the ensuing fire.

I had bought the Marina house in 1975, for about a hundred thousand. By 1989, it had ballooned in value to almost a half million. The insurance company paid off a hundred percent of the value, and another hundred stout for personal property, and I used the money to move into a Victorian on Russian Hill.

I like my house a lot. I can sit at the bay window in my kitchen and watch the marine traffic in the bay or move to my living room and catch a view of the Golden Gate and Mount Tam. It impresses the hell out of the women I bring there.

I quit the force shortly after buying the Russian Hill house and joined up in a private investigations firm owned by Jack Dobbs. Dobbs offered me a bonus for coming in, and then choked on his *coquille saint jacques* during a dinner at the Mark Hopkins three weeks later.

Fortunately, we had a contract.

The estate agreed that, in lieu of the money he owed me, I could have a little house he owned in Montara. It's not much, just two bedrooms, a bath and a half, a living room and kitchen, with redwood siding and a screened-in porch, but it's on the first row back from the beach, just across the PCH and up a little hill. I have an almost unspoiled view of the Pacific through the picture window at the front of the house, sullied only by the Chart House Restaurant, which somehow manages to stay open despite being situated in a backwater like Montara.

Highway 1 was blocked again south of the city, following some mudslides during the fall rains, so we had to take the scenic route through Daly City.

"Jesus," Taylor Chu said as we drove through the hills above the ocean. "I never get over what a crappy little town this is."

He was right. Developers moved into Daly City just after the war and threw up about six hundred cookie cutter split levels, not one of which varied in design from another. It was an ugly town.

Highway 1 opened up again in Pacifica, so I turned onto it and drove the last five miles to Montara.

I had decided to use the Montara estate as a sort of safe house for Chu. It had occurred to me that, since he was supposed to be dead and really wasn't, the folk who produced the ersatz corpse might be looking for him. Only a couple of people know about my Montara place.

After parking in the carport, out of the spill of light from the mercury lamps at the corner, I let Taylor Chu into my home away from home.

Just about everyone has the same reaction when they walk in. Since I don't live there much, there isn't much need to keep the place tidy. It's also where I indulge my hobby.

The living room is dominated by two workbenches. One is festooned with power tools - a twelve-inch drill press, fourteen-inch bench bandsaw, belt sander, and a jointer. The other bench holds my tool chest for sharps - chisels, gouges, and gravers, and the like. On one wall I installed a pegboard, from which hangs the various outside molds I use to build guitars, violins, lutes, and my current project, an Irish cittern.

I directed Taylor to the kitchen and asked him to bring a couple of beers into the living room. Meanwhile, I donned my denim shop apron, and placed a maple neck blank I had sawn to shape the other night into a bench vise.

I seated myself in my shop chair, braced the neck blank between my knees, and started peeling paper-thin slices of maple with a Kunz drawknife. Chu walked back in.

"What in hell is this?" he asked, as he handed me the beer.

"Helps me think," I said.

He looked around the room. On the wall across from the pegboard, I had installed hangers. On each one was a completed instrument. There was a copy of a pre-war Martin D-45 steel string guitar, a D'Angelico-style archtop jazz guitar I had finished a couple of months before, a ten-course lute, and a viola da Gamba I was particularly proud of, among others. Each one gleamed with multiple coats of lacquer, all hand-sprayed in my mini-barn out back of the house, except for the Martin copy, which was finished in satin shellac.

"Cool," Taylor said, as he looked them over. "You sell these?"

"If I sold them, it would become work," I said, placing the drawknife back on the bench and grabbing a concave spokeshave. "I already have a job. I do this to get away from it. I do give them away sometimes. If you're a good boy, I might let you have one."

"Do you play them all?"

"I'm learning. Each different type of instrument is tuned differently. Each one takes a whole new learning curve. We aren't here to talk lutherie, though."

Reality seemed to take hold again for him.

"No, I suppose not."

"Let's go through your story again, okay?"

He sat on the couch as I continued to shape the cittern neck.

"I was in my office, Thursday night," he began. "It was late. I always work late, it seems, at least for the last several years. Price of fame, I suppose."

Taylor Chu had made a number of headlines over the previous decade, defending various murder suspects from all over the Bay area. He had managed to get a decidedly generous number of them off. I had worked some of those cases, and a couple of them really had been innocent. I still had problems sleeping at night thinking about the ones he saved who really had needed a good whiff of the green gas, but his money was as good as anyone else's, and I had to make a living too.

"So I finished writing a couple of motions, packed up my briefcase so I wouldn't have to stop by the office before going to court the next day, and headed home.

"When I reached my car, two guys came up behind me while I was stowing the case in the trunk, and they threw some kind of blanket over my head. Next thing I knew, I was in the back of a pickup truck or a station wagon, maybe a van - it was open and wide, not like the trunk of a car - and we drove around for what seemed like hours."

"It always does," I said, drawing on my own unpleasant experience. "It's the adrenaline. It was probably only thirty minutes or so."

"Probably. Anyway, the vehicle finally stopped, and I was pulled out of it. There were more than two guys this time - lots of hands holding me, carrying me inside a building. It was stifling underneath that blanket. They had wrapped duct tape around my waist to pin it down and had secured my hands with some kind of plastic strap."

"Tie wraps. The kind of nylon self-locking cords used to hold cables together. The police have started using them instead of handcuffs in riot situations."

"I was placed in a small room. Pitch black. No sounds from outside, like it was soundproofed or something. Sometimes I could hear a muffled kind of murmur behind the door, like a couple of guys talking to each other, but I couldn't make out any words. I have no idea how long I was in there. I tried to sleep, until that got really weird. I'd wake up, but I had no way of knowing I was really awake. There was no division between day and night. I started hearing voices, people calling me from a distance. I could swear, at one point, I saw my ex-wife."

"Sensory deprivation," I said. "It's a brainwashing technique. Softens you up, makes you suggestible. Did they ever pipe in any music, or other sounds?"

"Not that I can recall. The sounds I thought I heard always seemed to come from inside me. Auditory hallucinations."

"You must have been in there a long time. What about food? Water?"

"I didn't get any while I was in the room, so I couldn't have been there more than a day or so. I remember being terribly hungry when I came out, and very thirsty. It was in the morning. Several people came for me, and dropped another blanket around my head. They carried me, but not far. A hundred yards or so, I'd say. They sat me in a hard wooden chair and took the blanket off my head. There was some food in front of me, on a television tray. It was fried fish, like that frozen stuff that you put in the oven, and some pork and beans. A glass of ice water, too. They told me not to turn around, and I heard them sneak away."

"The room was very large, about the size of a football field. It seemed to be like an old aircraft hangar or something. There were windows high on the walls, a lot of them broken. After I ate, I heard them coming for me again. They told me to sit still, and they threw the blanket over me. I was carried to another vehicle, or maybe it was the same one, I can't tell. This time they drove me for maybe twenty or thirty minutes. I couldn't be certain, but it seemed that we spent a long time going uphill, and then downhill again, like driving up and down a mountain. There were a lot of alternating right and left turns, so it could have been a mountain."

"The way these guys spoke," I asked, "Could you tell whether they were white, black, Asian?"

"Could have been Chinese," he said. "But you know as well as I do that second and third generation Asians have very little accent. I don't think they were black."

"So they drove you over the mountain?"

"That's the way it seemed. When the truck, van, whatever, finally stopped, they pulled me out and carried me back into some kind of building. I was given some more water to drink. It must have been drugged or something, because I became very sleepy. When I woke up, I was lying behind that dumpster on California Street."

"You didn't go straight to the cops?"

"That was my first thought. I started walking, trying to find a pay phone. When I got to the corner of California and Pine, though, I saw a newspaper in the rack. Nearly gave me a heart attack."

"It's not easy to wake up and find out you're dead," I said.

"Try it sometime. That's when I came straight to your office. It hadn't occurred to me to check my wallet, but when I did, it was gone. I guess that's how my driver's license wound up on the body of that fellow they threw off the bridge."

"Let's be precise," I suggested. "Let's refer to him as the fellow they killed, mutilated, and *then* threw off the bridge. Who do we both know who does that sort of thing?"

"Like you told that inspector. It sounds like the tongs to me."

I nodded and put the spokeshave back in the toolbox. A tidy shop is a happy shop.

I took a long swig of the beer. A relaxed PI is a happy PI.

I grabbed a full sheet of 80-grit garnet paper from a drawer of the workbench and folded it over the cittern neck. Grasping the ends, I started working the wood, like I was shining a pair of saddle oxfords, to make an even radius on the backside of the neck.

"So," I asked, "Just what are you involved in that would piss off the tongs? It isn't anything I've been working for you."

"That's the strange thing. I can't think of a case I'm in right now that involves them. Sure, I've defended some guys from down in Chinatown in the past, but none lately."

"See, it's like this," I said. "This is a kind of warning. The way I see it, they wasted someone expendable, and made it look like you, to send you a message."

"'It could have been me,'" he said.

"That would be the message. They're trying to scare you off something. And you have no idea what it might be?"

"None at all."

"Nothing really privileged that you don't want me to know about?"

"Everything I touch is equally privileged, Eamon. You know that. If I thought one of my cases had spurred this kidnapping and murder, I'd bring you in on it right away."

I finished with the 80-grit and replaced the garnet paper with some 120-grit silicon. The neck was smoothing nicely, and I took a moment to savor the figure emerging from the wood. It was rock maple, with some mild tiger-striping, and mottled with birdseye. I had already decided to french-polish this instrument. When I finished, it would be downright breathtaking.

I drained the beer and tossed the empty into a large plastic trashcan I kept next to the bench.

"I think you need to stay dead for a while," I said.

THREE

After assuring that Taylor was safely settled in for the night, I vacuumed the workshop and set the alarms. It was only eight or so, and I still had work to do.

I drove back into San Francisco, where I parked my car behind my office on Hyde Street. The first floor of my building is owned by Heidi Fluhr, who uses it for a small art gallery. I like the kind of stuff she sells—mostly representative paintings and the occasional nice piece of acrylic sculpture. She was still open when I parked the car.

I walked into the gallery and glanced around. Heidi was in the back, chatting up a couple of tourists who had wandered in between their visits to Pier 39 and Ghirardelli Square. I waited for them to leave.

Heidi closed the door behind them and locked it. Then she pressed her lips against mine and did a sort of locking thing there too. I liked that. Heidi had a way of doing things that just made me feel downright studly.

"Was that Taylor Chu I saw you drive away with earlier?" she said after separating with a satisfying lick.

"Yeah."

"Curious."

"You mean, him being dead and everything."

"That's what I was thinking."

"Yeah, it's curious."

"Curious enough that I shouldn't expect to see a retraction in the paper tomorrow?"

"Not quite that soon."

"Curious enough that you'd rather I didn't ask any more questions?"

I nodded

"This is gonna cost you, Gold," she said, as she twirled away to close out the register.

Heidi is one hundred percent Nordic stock - a big, healthy, blonde kid with breasts like honeydews and gymnast's legs that can squeeze the fight right out of you. For most guys, she's too tall and too strong. For me, she's just fine. She was wearing her hair pulled back and gathered with a ribbon, but as she cleared the register she yanked at the ribbon and this cascade of thick sun-drenched tresses just flowed around her shoulders like spilled milk running down a mountainside.

"Name your price," I said.

"I have been sitting here all day dreaming about a Dungeness crab from Nicks."

"Is he better in bed than me?"

She came around the counter in three big steps and wrapped her arms around my waist, pulling me close to her. We did the lingual mambo again for a minute or two, until we reached the limits of our mutual lung capacity.

"Baby," she said, "Take your time. Food first, fun later."

"Yes ma'am," I said, as she started stuffing the receipts into a bank bag.

I had started accompanying Heidi to the bank in the evenings several months earlier, after she had been tailed on the way to making the deposit at the night drop. I had figured, rightly, that some bad guy planned to relieve her of the bag and was casing her. Two nights later, I tailed the tail, and when he tried to make a move on her I showed him what a week in the hospital felt like. After that, I decided she could use a regular escort.

It had worked out nicely for both of us.

After making the night deposit, we strolled over to the wharf and slid into a booth at Nick's. Heidi had the Dungeness she had craved all day. I ordered a ribeye. I felt like a traitor, chowing down on beef when the catch of the day was stacked three deep in the iced bins outside the restaurant, but I tried not to let it ruin the gustatory excitement. Nick's makes a mean steak.

Heidi was very excited about a local artist she had collared that afternoon. He was doing some interesting things mixing oils and acrylic paint, to make his painting seem to fluoresce, and she had arranged to take eight of his larger works on consignment. She verbally rearranged the gallery as she ate.

I had other things on my mind, besides Heidi and Taylor Chu. While I had every intention of taking Heidi home to see if we couldn't set off a seismograph or two, it was destined to be a long evening.

The work of a private detective isn't much like the way it's portrayed on television. You spend a lot of time sitting in drab living rooms filled with ugly bric-a-brac, listening to some lonely old lady go on and on about her hammerhead nephew, when what you really wanted to know was whether she could identify the guy who crept into her bedroom window, tied her to the bedposts, and raped her repeatedly three weeks earlier. Denial is rampant among the masses. Sometimes you'd rather sit and listen to the nephew stories than deal with the pain your real questions will evoke.

Mostly, though, it's scut work. You walk from one bar to the next, showing pictures and asking questions, and huge portions of time are spent sitting in some doctor's waiting room for him or her to give you five minutes so you can ask about some client's injuries. Sometimes you just sit in a car and wait, often for the nothing that eventually happens.

That's why I charge by the hour and get expenses. Tonight, I had to do the bars.

––––––––––

Heidi was snoring peacefully when I extricated myself from her creamy arms and got dressed. I had never seen a girl so aroused by free crustaceans.

We had finished dinner and driven back to her apartment, a tidy thousand-dollar-a-month, four-hundred-square-foot job in North Beach. She was out of her clothes and scaling Mount Eamon almost before the door was locked.

It had been this way for several weeks, almost a ritual, and one I could get very used to. Neither of us, however, harbored any illusions that there was any permanence here. It was new and fun and rambunctious, and sooner or later we'd lick the red right off it and move on.

I was kind of hoping for *later.*

I leaned over to kiss her just before leaving, and she snuffled a bit and her eyes half-opened.

"Bye," she said, just like that, and rolled back over.

Some arrangement.

I let myself out and used a hidden key to secure the deadbolt.

I was working a skip trace for one of the local bail bondsmen. Kid named Cesar Ordonez had failed to appear in Superior Court on a car-boosting charge, and his bond was revoked. His bondsman, Doogie Portnoy, exercised the retainer I hold for him, and asked me to locate the kid.

A fellow I'd run into during the hunt told me that the Ordonez kid's closet had a revolving door, and he could often be found cruising the bars in the Tenderloin, South of Market.

I hate SoMa. I'd done my share of cruising there myself, back in my uniform days riding with Frank Raymond.

It's an amazing barrier, Market Street. You hop a cable car at the Hyde Street station near the wharf and ride it up to the top of the hill, and then down to Union Square, and all along the way you probably see happy, cheerful people with real lives, eating, talking, kissing, dancing. Then you get off at Union Square, and the sheer essence of pure commerce hits you like a wave of Santa Ana wind sweeping out of the desert.

Walk three blocks west, and you're in the middle of Beirut by the Sea.

SoMa can be a scary place. You cross Market and the price of your life goes down by half. Just turn the corner at Powell and Market, and walk toward the Bridge, and within seconds some vagrant will accost you, especially after dark. Keep walking, and you can feel the value of your skin draining like a punctured fuel tank.

Dark is when I work in this world, and that's why I hate SoMa.

I drove into the parking garage at the Nikko Hotel and pulled into the first space I saw. Before getting out of the car I reached into the glove compartment and grabbed the Browning nine I keep stashed there, and a small leather folding wallet containing my conceal permit. I know a lot of guys who have opted to go with foreign pieces - Glocks, Berettas, that sort of stuff. Me, I look for dependable. When, rarely, I have had occasion to yank steel out of my pants, I have always been thankful that I was strapped with American hardware. I've fired my weapon, maybe, five times in anger over the years. It hasn't refused to go *bang* yet.

I had installed a spring metal clip on the side of the Browning, so I didn't have to use a holster. I simply slipped the clip over my belt, and it stayed there ready for action. It was ten-thirty by the time I started hitting the bars. I crossed Market and made a beeline for the Tenderloin. The bars that side of town stay open until oh-dark-thirty, so I figured I had some time to work.

At each place, I'd pal up to the bartender and pull Ordonez's mug shot from my jacket pocket. Some recognized him, some didn't. None had seen him in the last couple of days.

I was in my eighth bar, a rancid place with badly stained carpet and music turned up just loud enough to puree your brain, showing my picture to the bartender. Some skinny Asian kid looked over my shoulder as I did it. I turned to him and looked as menacing as I could manage on six hours sleep in the last day and a half.

"Whatcha doon wit C-Note's pitcher, eh?" the kid asked. His eyes were glazed, and he had this shit-for-brains grin on his face. I figured it was Ecstasy, or maybe GBH, but I was on the clock, and didn't have time to hand out urine tests.

"You know this guy?" I asked.

The kid nodded, as he swayed to the insistent beat of the music.

"Yeah, I know him. C-Note, he calls hisself. He tricks."

So I'd heard.

"You trick?" I asked.

"When I gotta. Why? You lookin' for a little ac-tion?"

He stretched out the last word, like maybe he'd heard someone say on television.

"I'm looking for this guy. You know where he is? It'd be worth twenty."

"If it's worth twenty, it's worth forty."

I shook my head.

"If it's worth twenty, it's worth twenty. You know where he is, I figure there're fifteen other guys in here that do, too."

The kid seemed to sober up quickly.

"Twenty solid?"

"Yeah."

"I could be bullshittin' ya, man."

"And I could come back here and make it real hard for you to trick for a few weeks. Then I'd take my twenty back."

"You some kind of cop?"

"The kind who doesn't have to worry about a brutality beef. If you really know where C-Note's holing up, it's worth twenty to me. You don't, and you're thinking about shining me on, that would be a mistake."

The kid seemed to think about it for a second, but that was probably just my imagination. He didn't strike me as the thinking type.

"*Hola*, Paco!" the kid called to the bartender. "You got some paper I can write on?"

The bartender tossed a napkin at him. I pulled a pen from my jacket pocket. The kid scrawled an address on the paper.

"This is C-Note's ol' lady's place. She probably not at home right now, though, on account of she tricks too."

All God's children South of Market trick, I suppose. One big happy bunch of butt buddies.

I dropped a twenty on the bar for the kid, and a five for the bartender. All he'd supplied was the napkin, but I might be back some other time, and it never hurts to engender a little good will as you traverse this veil of tears.

The address on the napkin was a three-story house two blocks south. I could imagine what it looked like inside. Some enterprising sort had probably bought the house on the cheap years earlier, installed a few extra toilets, and had divided it up into six apartments. He charged five hundred a month each, and just raked in the money from it and twenty other tenements just like it as he sat in his plush office in the TransAmerica pyramid with his secretary kneeling in front of him making yummy sounds as she tried not to gag on his tool stuck halfway down her throat.

Or maybe I was just getting cynical.

There were two ways to do this. I could walk into the building, knock on some doors, wait to hit the right one, and then spend the next hour trying to stuff my intestines back into my body after Ordonez let loose with a deer load through the paper-thin door.

Plan B was I could hang out and wait for him to show his face, and hope he wasn't armed or accompanied by reinforcements.

I liked Plan B a lot better.

There was a pizza joint across the street from Ordonez' flop. I was still full from the dinner at Nick's, but I needed a cover. The place looked like hepatitis-to-go. I ordered a small cheese pie, and a large cola, and sat by the window alternating reading a Hispanic tossaway rag with taking small bites of the pizza and practicing my thirty chews which were supposed to result in excellent digestion.

The pizza wasn't all that bad, and I might have enjoyed it if I hadn't been full already. I nursed it for almost an hour, and smiled warmly at the counter clerk when he scowled at me for getting a refill on the drink.

While I wasn't reading or chewing, I had time to consider Taylor Chu's story. Something about it bothered me. I couldn't figure out the motivation for kidnapping him, holding him hostage, and then dumping him after faking his death. There was no ransom involved, as far as I could tell.

He denied any case involvement with the tongs, but that didn't necessarily mean anything.

Take a hike across Grant Avenue, and you might think you're in a summer stock revival of *Flower Drum Song*, but that's just window dressing. Every shop owner east of Pacific is paying protection dues to one tong or another. It's called *lai-see,* or lucky money, a sort of gang version of the money given to children on Chinese New Year. You pay it, and you don't run out of luck. You can't order an egg roll at a corner Takee Outee without some gangster skimming his cut.

It's a nice arrangement, though. The protection you buy is real, not the ponied-up kind you might get paying off a couple of bent-nosed types in Brooklyn or Detroit. When they say you're protected, they mean against anything - especially the other tongs. There's a paternalistic relationship between the gangs and the working-class Chinese down there. Sometimes, though, you don't have a clue whose toes you're stepping on.

Still, I couldn't figure out the reasons behind snatching Chu and then turning him loose. The message angle sounded good, but someone had to pay the freight with his hands, feet, and head. That's quite a lot of trouble to go through to get your point across.

I was still tussling with my discomfort over the Chu case when Ordonez made his appearance. It was a good thing I hadn't gone hunting inside the apartment building, because he hadn't been there.

Around one in the morning, he walked into the pizza place.

I was reasonably certain we hadn't met, but when you hang around the courts and police stations as much as I do you never know. I rustled the paper and stuffed my face with food as he boogied into the joint.

He ordered a garbage pie in street-accented Spanglish, and jitterbugged around the shop while he waited for it to cook. He would drop fifty cents into a video game, leave it halfway finished, then stand at the counter and beat out a salsa rhythm with his fingertips. He was like the National Crankhead Poster Child.

Finally, the pizza was done. He paid the counter clerk, and floated out the door, across the street, and up the steps of his building.

At this point, I had a chance to do something really shady. A lot of peepers I know would have done it. Portnoy had retained my services, and I was working through the up-front money. It wasn't much, just five notes. I can run through that in a decent day, easy. By my clock, he was about two hours away from using up the retainer. When it was gone, he had a choice of paying me off or retaining me again. Portnoy and I go back a few years, and it's been a good working relationship, but that doesn't mean I couldn't stand a few extra hundred in my pocket. You see, when a guy like Portnoy retains my services, it isn't like I put the money in a jar and take it out as it's used. I have ongoing expenses just like anyone else. By the time I get around to earning off the retainer, it's usually already long gone.

I had a feeling Ordonez was settling in for the night. Maybe he planned to snarf through the pizza while checking out an old Shirley Temple movie on AMC, and then crash. Whatever the case, I didn't expect to see him again before, say, noon. I could hang out in the neighborhood for a couple of hours, bill them back to Portnoy, and come out of it with six hundred more dollars - a hundred for my time, and five for a new retainer.

Like I said, a lot of guys would have done it. A lot do. It was this sort of dilemma that was aging me prematurely.

I pulled the cell phone out of my jacket pocket.

Now here's another difference between me and Magnum P.I.. Ol' Mag, at this point, would ring Rick and T.C. to back him up, and then go upstairs for a little *mano a mano* with C-Note. I'm still amazed that he lived through six seasons on television. The way I see it, Portnoy's five bills were nowhere near enough incentive to take a chance on getting my nose laid over by some on-the-lam wetback cranker. There was an easier way.

Since Ordonez had missed his trial date, there was a fugitive warrant out for him. When I pulled out the cell phone, I dialed the preset for the Tenderloin division of SFPD. As a concerned citizen, I informed the friendly, helpful dispatch clerk there that a dangerous wanted felon was holed up across the street from me, and then I just sat back and waited for the late show to commence.

Maybe half an hour later, which was pretty good for this part of town, a bubbletop pulled up in front of Ordonez' dump. Seconds later, another pulled in behind it. Four guys went upstairs. Five came down, one of them loud, abusive, and underdressed.

I made another telephone call, this time to Portnoy, to inform him that his skip had been traced. I still had an hour and a half left on his retainer. Honesty had cost me six hundred dollars.

On the other hand, I didn't have to spend another hour and a half on the SoMa side of the Tenderloin.

Things balance out.

FOUR

I slept in the next morning, until about nine. After showering and shaving, I stopped by a bakery on the way to work and grabbed half a dozen doughnuts and couple of coffees.

I got to the office just as Heidi was opening the gallery.

"Breakfast?" I said as I slid out of the car.

"I don't know," she said. "Look what I had to do for dinner."

I followed her into the gallery and waited for her to put the start-up money in the cash register. While she did that, I poured sugar and cream into the coffee, just the way she had led me to believe she liked it.

"What in hell did you do to me last night?" she asked as she reached into the bag for a cruller. "My cookie's sore."

"That would be a number thirty-seven," I said.

"You have them labeled?"

"You know how it is. After a while, there are patterns."

"Routines."

"More or less."

"Yeah, it did seem pretty routine at that. What in hell are you doing out of bed this time of the morning?"

"Errands."

"Any of them involving the not-quite-dead Taylor Chu?"

"I thought I bought your silence with a Dungeness crab last night."

She sat on the stool behind her counter and pouted. I had to hold myself back from committing an act of public indecency.

"I mean it," I said. "You can't talk about Chu. If I'd imagined you might see him with me last night, I would have taken greater care. You read the papers. You know what they did to that guy they tossed off the bridge."

"Oh, ick."

"It wasn't any fun for him, either. Do us both a favor and keep the Chu thing under your hat."

She smiled and nodded. Heidi was just shy of thirty, and she didn't know shit about what could happen to her on the streets. She knew acrylics and oils and watercolors, and she could actually talk for half an hour on the distinctions between Monet and Manet, but she didn't understand the ugly stuff. For her it was all television and lurid novels. It was important to me that she at least understood the meaning of *keep it zipped*.

"What are you doing for dinner tonight?" she asked.

"I'm still working on breakfast. What did you have in mind?"

"Call me later. I'll work on a craving."

The door to the gallery opened, and an Asian woman walked in. She was a head shorter than Heidi, maybe five-six, and she was dressed in a conservative suit with sensible heels, her hair pulled back in a severe bun. She wore large advertising executive glasses. Her makeup was professionally applied and expertly understated. She had tried very hard to look businesslike and very uptown, but the way she moved betrayed an earthier, more sensuous personal life. Heidi stiffened immediately, in a way I'd only seen previously in threatened cats.

"Excuse me," she asked Heidi. "I'm looking for the man in the office upstairs. Mr. Gold?"

I stepped forward and offered my hand.

"I'm Eamon Gold," I said. "I was just bringing Ms. Fluhr a snack. Can I help you?"

She glanced back and forth from me to Heidi.

"Perhaps you'd like to step up to my office?" I offered.

"That would be fine."

I gestured for our visitor to step outside the gallery to take the center stairs up to the second floor. As I followed her out, I turned back to Heidi and pulled my fingers across my lips, reminding her to stay quiet about Chu.

She stuck her tongue out at me.

I followed my visitor up the stairs and unlocked the door to my office. She took a seat in the chair directly across from my desk. I slid around her and took my seat.

"My name is Wei Ma Lo," she said.

"How can I help you, Ms. Wei?"

"I am trying to find my brother."

"What's his name?" I said, pulling out a legal pad to make some notes.

"Wei Ping Yun, but he goes by the name Buddy."

"Buddy Wei?"

"Yes."

I got her address and phone number and asked her to tell me all she could about her brother.

"Buddy is twenty-three. He lives with me. Our father died three years ago. Four nights ago, he left the apartment to go to a movie."

"Which movie?"

She named an action flick starring a Hong Kong stalwart who was starting to hit it big in the USA.

"Was he going to a theater in Chinatown, or somewhere else?"

"I don't know. He just said he was going to the movie. He didn't come home that night, but that wasn't unusual. When he didn't return by the next evening, I became worried. By the day after that, I was concerned. He is still missing."

"You've contacted the police?"

"No."

I shifted in my seat. I could see what was coming next.

"You're undocumented?"

She became visibly uncomfortable.

"Look, Ms. Wei, I'm not a cop, and I don't work for the INS. I don't particularly care if you're a citizen or not. Your money's as green as anyone else's."

"I was afraid to go to the police," she explained.

"What about your tong?"

She became really alarmed.

"I do not understand," she said.

"Yeah you do. The Triads are all over Chinatown. The only way you could have gotten into this country and gotten settled was with their assistance. It would have cost a ton for all of you - your father and brother and yourself - to come over. I figure the Snakehead gangs charged around a hundred thousand."

She lowered her head and stared at the floor.

"I have not contacted the block manager," she said. "We did not have the money to pay in advance for our... our trip. The man who arranged for us to come here recruited Buddy. He has been working for him... them."

"What kind of work?"

"Running errands. Making deliveries. He worked for a moving company owned by Sung Chow Li, and there was a lot of work."

Now I settled back in my seat. The minute she mentioned Sung Chow Li, things started to come together.

"Is it possible, Ms. Wei, that Buddy is on a job for Mr. Sung? Maybe he's doing a cross-country move, and just hasn't bothered to call. Maybe he hasn't had a chance to get in touch."

"I suppose it is possible," she said.

"But you haven't contacted the block manager for Mr. Sung."

"No," she said. I saw a single tear fall from her downcast face and plop on the summer wool jacket she was wearing.

"What are you afraid of, Ms. Wei?"

She didn't say anything. I waited for almost a minute, and three tears.

"Do you have a tissue?" she said finally.

I dug around in a desk drawer until I found a half-empty box of wipes. I handed it to her across the desk.

"Okay," I said. "I get the picture. You can't go to the police because you're afraid they'll hand you over to Homeland Security. You can't go to Mr. Sung, because you're afraid of him for some reason. You want me to nose around and see if maybe Buddy's just off on a job, or maybe he really has gone missing."

"Yes," she said, dabbing at the corner of her eye with the tissue.

"This could be cheap, if all I have to do is make a call on Mr. Sung. On the other hand, it could get expensive."

"How much do you need?"

"It's seventy an hour, plus expenses. Expenses include anything I spend while I'm working on your case. That means gasoline, food, entertainment for possible leads, even bullets if I have to use them."

She looked up at that.

"I'm joking," I said. "I almost never charge for the bullets."

Which was more or less correct, since I almost never used them.

"I'd need five hours in advance," I said. "That's three hundred fifty."

She pulled a wallet from her purse and fished through it. She handed over four hundred-dollar bills. I looked at them. They were new. The numbers were sequential.

I pulled out my money clip and handed over two twenties and a ten. Then I pulled out my receipt book and wrote her a note for the advance.

"Is there anything else you need?" she asked.

"Plenty. Let's start with a picture of your brother, and then a list of all of Buddy's friends...."

Wei Ma Lo left after I filled a couple of pages of the legal pad with notes.

I had a lot of ideas where Buddy Wei might have wound up, but I didn't tell her any of them, because she already seemed to be having a lousy day.

I locked up the office, asked Heidi to keep a lookout for visitors, and drove to Montara.

There was a quarter hour delay in Pacifica, because of the construction to repair Highway 1. I spent the time cruising through the talk radio channels, looking for any mention of

Taylor Chu. Sure enough, there was a discussion on KSFO on gang violence in Chinatown, and his name was a central feature of the discussion. It seemed that Frank Raymond and I weren't the only ones who saw the tongs behind this one.

Chu was sitting on the couch, reading a book, when I finally got to the Montara house. The temperature at the beach was easily twenty degrees higher than in the city, and the house was getting a little close.

"Sorry," I said, as I adjusted the automatic thermostat. "I forgot to show you how to change the settings. I have this thing programmed to turn off at eight in the morning. By one, you'd have been roasting."

When I hit "Run Program", the air conditioner immediately kicked in, and there was a gentle whoosh of air from the registers set in the ceiling.

"What did you find out?" he asked.

"Nothing. I did a skip trace until about two this morning, and I had a client sign-up this morning. I plan to get on your case this afternoon. Might be able to kill two birds with one stone."

I sat at the workbench and pulled a couple of engraving files from my tool chest. The cittern neck was sitting just where I had left it. I had roughed it out, but I still needed to carve a volute underneath the headstock. I chucked it in the leather-jawed bench vise and pulled on a pair of high-powered reading glasses so I could work in close. Slowly, I started filing away the basic shape of the volute.

"How's that?" he asked.

"Kid who visited me today is looking for her brother. Seems he works for Sung Chow Li."

"What's that have to do with me getting kidnapped?"

"There are seven tongs, Taylor. Sung runs one of them. If I start nosing around looking for this kid, I might as well ask some questions about you, too."

"You think Sung may have been behind it?"

"I don't know. I won't know until I start digging around. That's the way it works. I ask questions, and someone gives me an answer. I take the answer and formulate some more questions. Sooner or later, the answers start to form a pattern. The pattern tells me something."

"What if someone tries to stop you?"

"Tells me I asked someone the right question. For instance, did any of your cases involve Sung Chow Li?"

"Directly? No. You know how it is, though. You take a case in Chinatown, and sooner or later you're going to run up against a tong member."

"Any of your clients work high up in the Sung organization?"

"Not currently. Some in the past."

"The ones you worked for in the past - did you win?"

"What's that got to do with it?"

"If you lost, they might hold a grudge. Or, if you represented one of Sung's most trusted in an action involving one of the other tongs and won, then maybe you pissed off that group. Grabbing you took some organization, coordination, planning. This wasn't one disgruntled guy acting out a grudge. I don't see this coming down to that."

He settled back on the couch, a deliberative, thoughtful look on his face.

"Man, this is confidential shit, Eamon."

"And I work for you. You pull me in on the case, as the lead investigator, and confidentiality isn't an issue. For instance, what were you working on the night you were nabbed?"

"I had a first appearance in court the next day. It was a court appointed case—public defender stuff."

"Aren't you kind of pricey for that kind of thing?"

"It happens. If you're hanging around the courtroom when a case comes up, and a defendant asks for a CA lawyer, sometimes the judge just assigns it to you on the spot."

"You have to accept?"

"These are judges, Eamon. They can tell you what color your shit has to be the next day, and you'd better comply. So, I was hanging out in Fred Garmon's courtroom last week, waiting to file a continuance, and they bring this kid in from the jail. Couldn't have been more than seventeen, eighteen years old from the look of him. His name was Chong Lin Kow. He was arrested on an assault charge—deadly weapon, intent to kill—at an illegal rave bar two nights earlier."

"If he's tonged up, why didn't he already have a lawyer?"

"He isn't involved in any of the local tongs. Kid's a newcomer, just arrived from someplace back east, DC area. He doesn't even live in Chinatown. Has a flop over in the Castro."

"Is he gay?"

"What difference does that make?"

"All kinds, when it comes to motive."

"I don't know. I didn't ask."

"So he went to this after-hours raver and wound up in a fight."

"Place was set up in a closed cold-storage over near Pier 53. It's the kind of place they like to take over. From what I could gather, it was all really mellow, lots of underage kids lying around on couches zonked on designer drugs, some music playing. Chong, though, he somehow got his hands on

some crack, and he and a couple other kids smoked it in the
alley next to the building."

"Rave clubs aren't known for hard drug use."

"What can I say? Kid's from out of town. One thing leads
to another, and he gets into a fight with another kid, guy
named Fat Wa something or other - I don't have my notes.
Can't recall. Chong grabs a stick off the ground and starts
wailing on this Fat kid. Beats him to a bloody pulp. Someone
calls the cops, probably one of the fellows who set up the
rave. These guys like to keep a low profile, and they're quick
to call the cops if something goes wrong. So, the cops get
there. They find Chong leaning up against the side of the
building, and Fat is just this big heap of highway hamburger
on the sidewalk. Fat goes to the hospital, and Chong goes to
jail."

"What do you know about this kid, Fat Wa whatever?"

"Not much. It was just a first appearance. I had planned
on getting Chong to plead down to simple, maybe walk with
a fine. He didn't have a record, so what the hell?"

"Okay, so I check out Chong and Fat. Anything else?"

"Nothing big. There's a contract thing I'm doing."

I placed the files back in the toolbox and pulled out a
couple of knives. I really like my knives. I bought them at a
trade show. They were made from surgical steel, reground,
formed and sharpened to a razor keen, and then placed in
some beautiful *bois de rose* handles. The rosewood had an
agreeable, oily feel as I pulled the knives from the toolbox.
One was a straight blade. The other was curved to a
hawksbill point. I started alternating them to bring some
definition to the volute. Later, I'd hit it with a very narrow
veining gouge.

"I didn't think you did contracts."

"It's for a friend. Sherman Fong."

"Restaurant guy."

"Yeah. Sherman and I grew up together. We've been friends for thirty years."

"What's the contract?"

"Nothing unusual. He's branching out, taking on a partner for a new venture. They just needed to have some stuff in writing."

"Who's the partner?"

"His name's Barney Gates. He has a couple of steak houses in Sacramento and Richmond. He wants to set up shop in San Francisco, Cow Hollow. Apparently Sherman's looking at the same thing, so they decided to joint venture."

"Doesn't sound like there's anything there."

"That's why I didn't mention it."

"I'll check out this guy Gates anyway. You never know. Mind if I take a look at Fong?"

"That's the nice thing about being dead," Chu said as he stretched out on the couch. "Nothing much gets to you anymore. You ask anyone anything you want, Eamon. You jangle a few nerves, I figure I can throw oil on the water later."

FIVE

Wei Ma Lo had given me five names of guys she knew to be Buddy Wei's friends. I decided to start off talking with them.

The first one lived in a third-floor walkup over a Chinese novelties shop on Pacific Avenue. Since I was going to be doing a lot of in and out over the course of the afternoon, I left the car behind the gallery on Hyde Street and took the bus. San Francisco is a wonderful city, but it was not built for heavy automobile traffic. Finding a parking space in the middle of the day in Chinatown is a genuine hassle. Mass transit in the city is actually pretty good, and I didn't have to worry about parking tickets.

The bus let me off at the corner of Grant and Pacific, and I walked the two blocks to Sammy Chin's apartment.

The stairs were filthy, and the hallway smelled like a pig had eaten raw sewage and died. Each hallway had a single light bulb in the ceiling, which created spooky shadows as I walked from the stairway to Chin's rooms.

I banged on the door. For a moment, I thought nobody was home. Then, I heard the rasp of the deadbolt being thrown.

The door opened about three inches, as far as the chain allowed, and I back away as the sweet acrid smell of marijuana slammed through the crack.

"What?" said a young woman.

I handed her my card.

"What's this?"

My eyes adjusted and I realized the woman was a girl, no more than sixteen. She was wearing a pair of pink flowered panties. That's it. Just the panties.

"My business card. I'm looking for Sammy Chin."

"Wha'd he do?"

"Nothing. He's a friend of a guy I'm looking for. I just want to ask him some questions."

"Who's this guy you looking for?"

"Is Sammy Chin in?" I asked.

"No. He's at work."

"Can you tell me where he works?"

This was getting tedious.

"You go there, you'll get him in trouble."

"I don't want to cause problems for him. I'll be careful. Where's he work?"

"Sung Moving," she said, dreamily. Then she closed the door in my face.

It made sense, I suppose. A lot of these Chinese illegals work like dogs, sometimes fifteen, sixteen hours a day. It stands to reason that they'd associate primarily with working companions.

I decided to forego visits to the other four guys on my list, and instead paid a visit to Sung Moving.

It wasn't so much a business as it was a parking lot. Sung Moving was situated on the outer boundaries of Chinatown, over near North Beach. There were three big panel trucks parked in the lot, concealing a small, former gas station, in which a young woman wearing jeans, high-heeled clogs, and a muscle shirt sat behind a desk. She didn't wear a bra, and I could make out the concentric circles of her nipples through the fabric of the shirt. She was Hispanic. She had colored her hair this atrocious shade of reddish brown, and had carried the theme to her face, where her eye shadow did little to accentuate her Castilian eyes.

She had rings in her ears, eyelid, and nose. When she opened her mouth, I could see the stud in her tongue. Her lips were painted three shades - red, brown, white, in another set of concentric lines. She looked like a sideshow geek I had seen at the fair when I was a kid, but that might just be my middle-aged brain talking. Overall, she wasn't much different than half the girls I ran into in this city.

"Sammy Chin?" I asked as I laid my card on the desk in front of her. She ignored it.

"Who wants him?"

I poked at the card on the desk.

"Oh, yeah," she said, after glancing at it. "He in trouble?"

"You're the second person to ask that. Is he likely to be in trouble?"

The question apparently contained too many words for her, because she just bobbed her head and stared at me, the way a fish looks at its reflection in the aquarium glass.

"Is he around?"

"Out on a job," she said.

I supposed I was going to have to limit my questions to three short words.

"When's he back?"

"Don't know. He in trouble?

Oh, brother.

I pulled out my notepad, onto which I had transcribed the information I'd gotten from Wei Ma Lo.

"What about Gow Li Peng?"

For a second, I was worried that I might have violated the word limit.

"Oh, you mean Lanny!"

"That his nickname?"

"I dunno. I just recognized the name from his paycheck. We call him Lanny. Can't remember all those Chinese names."

"So, is Lanny around?"

"He's out with Sammy."

This was taking on all the urbanity of a George and Gracie routine, so I decided to go for broke.

"What about Buddy Wei?"

"Oh, he don't work here no more."

Now we were getting somewhere.

"Since when?"

"He quit about two weeks ago. I wrote him out his last check - what? - Monday. He ain't picked it up yet."

"Would you mind if I took a look at the check?"

She got up and rummaged around in a file cabinet behind the desk. She pulled out a file and flipped through it. Finally, she pulled out a sheet of paper with a check attached.

The paper was a release. It stated that Buddy Wei would not hold Sung Moving responsible for any further disbursement of funds, and that he had about two thousand dollars tied up in a retirement fund. He had several choices of what to do with the money, including just leaving it in the fund to grow like Topsy.

The check was for almost seven hundred dollars.

"He hasn't come by for the check?" I asked.

"No. But it's just since Monday. Maybe he went out of town."

"That's a lot of money to leave lying around. If I were going out of town, I might want to take it with me."

Clearly, the girl hadn't given it all that much thought. She just stared again. Perhaps she was only capable of responding to direct questions.

"Wouldn't you?" I asked, completing the thought.

"I guess."

See? I was figuring out the rules as we went along.

"I know Mr. Sung owns this business, but who's the manager?"

"Huh?"

"Your boss. What's his name?"

"Oh, that's Mr. Loo."

"His first name?"

"No, that's his last name."

"I mean..." I sighed and thought about all my tax money going to the public education system. "What's Mr. Loo's first name?"

"Chuck."

"Chuck Loo," I said, as I wrote the name in my notebook. "Has Mr. Loo been around lately?"

"Not since Monday. He came in to sign the checks."

I put the notebook away. All in all, despite the girl's vapid responses, I had learned a thing or two.

"Thanks," I said, and started to leave.

"Should I tell Sammy you were looking for him?" she asked.

"Don't bother."

The bus dropped me off in front of the Holiday Inn at Fisherman's Wharf, and I walked the block and a half to my office.

Heidi was occupied with five or six customers in the gallery, so I walked right past her door and took the stairs to my office.

The first thing I noticed was that my door was open.

I thought for a second about the Browning in my glove compartment and considered going to grab it before entering the office. At that moment, though, two men walked out onto the landing.

"Mr. Gold?" one of them asked. They were Asian, and I would have bet on Chinese even before he spoke.

"I don't suppose either one of you guys is Buddy Wei." I said.

They looked at one another, and for a moment I thought I saw a glimmer of concern cross the speaker's face.

He turned back to me and reached into his jacket pocket. I imagined him coming out with an Uzi or something, and considered dashing back down the stairs, but then I would have just gotten blood all over the sidewalk, and that would have killed Heidi's business for the rest of the afternoon.

He pulled out a business card. I liked that a lot better than a gun.

I reached up and took the card.

It read, *Sung Chow Li Enterprises.*

"Mr. Sung has asked us to invite you to meet with him," the speaker said.

"Regarding...?"

"He didn't confide in me. Would you like to come with us?"

I didn't like the idea a bit. On the other hand, I did feel pretty certain that there was a gun close to where the card came from, and I was also relatively assured that the other fellow was strapped too. That made it two firearms to none

That sweetened their invitation some.

"Sure," I said.

"We have the car parked behind the building."

I walked down the stairs with them in tow. The speaker pointed to the side of the building, and I followed them to a gray Lincoln Town Car. It glittered in the sunlight reflecting off the bay. The quiet guy opened the rear door and gestured for me to slide in.

"Mind if I sit in front?" I asked. He gave me this quizzical look.

The speaker said something to him in Chinese, and he nodded, closed the door, and opened the passenger side door in front. I wished I could understand what they said, but I had taken the advice of a poly-sci professor in college who had said that optimists learn Russian, and pessimists learn Chinese. I took a seat and nearly sank into the plush leather upholstery. Quiet Dude took the seat behind me.

The fellow who had done all the talking got behind the wheel, and I was on my way back to Chinatown.

Somehow, they had no problem finding a parking spot right in front of Sung's offices.

They let me out of the car, and made me the meat in a Chinese sandwich, as we walked into Sung's offices.

I don't know what I expected, but it looked very much the way any office might. There was a receptionist, and down a short hall I could see a cube farm, the topographic signature of the modern corporation. The walls were tastefully finished in grasscloth, and the carpet was a utilitarian short pile, made for heavy traffic.

They led me to an elevator, which we took to the fourth floor. It opened directly into a large office dominated by an immense walnut desk at one end, an indoor koi pond to the right, and a bank of windows opening out onto the street below to the left.

The boys walked me over to a row of leather-covered seats facing the desk and indicated that I should sit.

Then they left the room.

I sat there, trying not to hyperventilate, until I heard a door close somewhere behind the desk. A door at the back of the room opened, and Sung Chow Li walked in.

He crossed to me, extending his hand.

"Mr. Gold?" he said.

"Eamon Gold," I said.

"A pleasure, sir."

He grasped my hand and shook vigorously.

"Please," he said, gesturing toward the chair, "have a seat."

He walked behind his desk and sat in a high-backed, rolled and pleated leather executive's chair, talking all the time.

"I'm sorry for what must look like strong-arm tactics, but I have been trying to contact you all day. I have just called my employees waiting for you at your home. I assure you, you won't be bothered again."

"What can I do for you, Mr. Sung?"

"Well, this is a rather... delicate matter. It has to do with Taylor Chu."

I nodded, but I didn't say anything.

"I was wondering if you might give him a message for me."

"Wouldn't that be a little difficult?"

Sung grinned.

"A joke, eh? Yes, I suppose it would be difficult, if in fact it were Mr. Chu's body that was found in the bay. Of course, we both know it wasn't, don't we?"

"Tell me more," I urged.

"Ah, yes. Detective's tricks. I have nothing to hide. I know Taylor Chu is alive. Sooner or later, I expect that he will contact you. I was hoping you would give him a message for me."

"On the off chance he reappears, what's the message?"

"Tell him, it wasn't me."

"What wasn't you?"

"Any of it. Mr. Chu is a very powerful man, Mr. Gold, even if he himself denies it. When he contacts you, he is likely to tell an amazing story. I just want him to know I had nothing to do with it. I may have need of Mr. Chu's services in the future, and I wouldn't want to prejudice him against me."

I waited for more.

Nothing seemed to be coming.

"Is... is that it?" I asked.

"It would mean a lot to me if you would pass it along," Sung said.

"May I ask whether you know whom Mr. Chu might contact to express his gratitude for not being dead?"

Sung smiled. Maybe he was just amused by my lousy syntax.

"Mr. Chan has an envelope," he pointed toward my escort, the one who had done all the talking. "It is compensation for your time. I regret bringing you here without some advance notice, or issuing a more formal invitation, but time, I felt, was of the essence."

"I'll make certain that Mr. Chu gets the message the next time I see him," I said. "If there's nothing else..."

I started to get up from the chair. Nobody stopped me. I turned to walk toward the elevator, the door of which was flanked by the guys who had brought me to the meeting. Halfway across the floor, I stopped.

I turned back toward Sung.

"Excuse me, Mr. Sung, but there is another matter, a completely different situation. I have been asked to find a young man whom I believe works for you. Buddy Wei?"

Sung got the same look Chan had given me from the top of my stairs. Something about Wei troubled him greatly. He recovered just as quickly, however, and the ingratiating smile returned to his face.

"I'm sorry, Mr. Gold, but I'm afraid I don't know the name of every person who works in my various companies."

"He's with Sung Moving. I was there earlier today. Apparently he quit a couple of weeks ago..."

"Well, there you are..."

"But he hasn't been by to pick up his last paycheck. The girl I spoke with there also said the manager, Mr. Loo, hasn't been by since the first of the week."

"Mr. Loo is on a delivery, Mr. Gold. He is handling a move by one of my associates to Los Angeles. I expect that he will return by the end of the weekend. As for Mr. Wei..." he shrugged.

"Well, thank you, sir," I said, and turned to go again.

Despite his relatively pleasant appearance, I thought I could feel his eyes boring into me all the way to the elevator door. I had rocked him a little when I mentioned Buddy Wei, just as I had Chan. He knew who Wei was, all right, but it didn't suit his purposes to admit it.

Chan slipped me an envelope as I got back into the Lincoln. As he walked around to the driver's side, I peeked inside. I counted ten pictures of Benjamin Franklin before he opened the door and I had to stop.

It was comforting, and a little disturbing, to realize I hadn't counted nearly all of them.

Whatever Sung thought he was buying with the money, it was for certain a lot more than a messenger boy.

Chan dropped me off at the gallery. It was now long past lunchtime, to the point that I decided I'd just tough it out until dinner.

Heidi was directing a couple of moving men who were struggling with some large canvasses, trying to get them through the door to her shop. I had a feeling she was going to eventually have to use the shipping entrance in the back, but she seemed single-minded about using the front.

Maybe she wanted the paintings to make a grand entrance.

I just winked at her and started up the stairs to my office. She blew me a kiss, so I guess she had forgiven my dalliance with Wei Ma Lo.

I sat at my desk for a long time, trying to sort it all out.

Buddy Wei had come into the country illegally, which probably put him into debt to Sung Chow Li to the tune of almost thirty grand. He had gone to work for Sung's moving business, and I would have been flabbergasted if his paycheck didn't include a substantial deduction for 'loan repayment'.

One thing was certain. Buddy was in for a lifetime of repaying. The money he owed Sung came with a healthy vigorish, one that would never be touched by the minimum payment. Unless Buddy Wei invented teleportation, or a cure for cancer, or something else that made him insanely wealthy, he was going to be in debt for the rest of his life.

So, why did he quit Sung Moving? Even I, an intellectually-limited round-eyes, knew that once the tongs got their hooks in you, you stayed hooked. He wouldn't be allowed to just up and quit, unless it was to move on to another of Sung's operations.

That meant that either Buddy Wei was still working for Sung, or he was on the run. Once he quit his job, someone was bound to come looking for him to pay up on his debt. The only way out of that situation was to hit the road hard and fast, and not stop running.

If that were the case, I'd run through every penny Wei Ma Lo had, and never even get a sniff of her lost brother.

The other thing I'd learned, however useful it was, was that Sung Chow Li was afraid of Taylor Chu. Sung had made a point of getting the message to Chu that he hadn't been behind the kidnapping. Sung was worried that Taylor might try to take it out on him. That also meant that Sung had reason to believe that Chu would blame him for the snatch.

I made a note to discuss this with my client at the first available opportunity.

My day was only half over, though. I still had to check out Chong Kow, his beating victim Fat Wa Whatever, and maybe get some information on Barney Gates.

Since I was bucks up, thanks to Sung, I took a cab down to the Civic Center, at Polk and Van Ness. The county clerk's office is situated there, and that's where they keep the court records. I have a friend there.

Shirley Jones (no, not *that* one) was seated behind her desk, sipping on a cup of coffee and removing staples from a stack of papers when I sauntered into her office. At first she didn't look up. Then she did. Then she scowled at me.

"What in hell are you doing here?" she asked.

This is how a lot of my friends greet me. After a while you learn to let it roll off your back.

"Have I missed something?"

"About a month ago, remember? You were supposed to take me to the opening of the Degas exhibit?"

"I was in the hospital, Shirl."

"I know. It was inconsiderate, going out and getting yourself beaten up like that, when you knew you had a commitment. I had to scrounge around for a date. Wound up with that spooky guy Neil from accounting."

"Would it help if I were to apologize?"

"No."

"Okay. So I won't. How about this? I'm bucks up right now. Why don't we take in a 49ers game next week?"

"You can get tickets?"

"I know a guy."

Actually, I knew a whole bunch of guys.

She seemed temporarily mollified.

"What do you want, Eamon?"

I pulled the notebook from my jacket pocket and flipped through a couple of pages.

"I need the date of an assault case. Kid named Chong Lin Kow."

"That with a C or a K?"

"It's K." I scribbled the name on a sheet of the paper, along with the partial name of his victim, Fat Wa whatever. I ripped it out of the notebook and handed it to her.

She punched a number of keys on her computer and waited.

"It's been disposed," she said.

"Beg pardon?"

"Went to trial on Friday last week. Your kid Chong pled down, got a fine, and was released. The victim's name was Fat Wa Loo."

"Wait a minute," I said. "How did it go to court? His attorney was missing."

She looked up at me, pulled her reading glasses down her nose, and leaned back in her chair.

"This was one of Taylor Chu's cases?"

"Chu picked it up in court as a *pro bono.*"

"Well, apparently someone else picked it up on Friday morning when Chu didn't show up for the hearing."

"Any way to find out who the attorney was?"

"Not in this file. Hold on."

She picked up the telephone and dialed five digits, an interoffice number.

"Hey, Brian, this is Shirley.... Not bad, you?... Well, take a lot of vitamin C... Yeah, I need some information on who represented a kid in court last Tuesday..." She picked up the sheet of paper and read from it. "Chong Lin Kow... Yeah, a K... Assault with intent, pled down to simple...Okay, thanks."

She wrote a name down on the slip of paper and handed it to me.

Under Fat Wa Loo's name, she had written *Louis Gai.*

I knew Louis Gai. We had crossed paths several times, usually in court when I was forced to testify about my methods in obtaining evidence. It's not generally well known, but the cops aren't the only ones bound by the Fourth Amendment. If I go into some guy's house and just run across evidence of illegal behavior, it may not be admissible, since I might not have had probable cause to believe it was there.

Louis Gai was an expert on the Fourth Amendment. He used it the way some thugs use a sap, to beat witnesses about the head and shoulders until they yell *Uncle.* His clients walk on technicalities maybe eighty percent of the time. He represents a lot of mokes from Chinatown. It is fairly common knowledge that he has a good working relationship with most of the tongs.

So, Taylor Chu gets nabbed, and immediately Louis Gai steps into the ring to take his place.

I had an idea.

"Shirl, could you raise a rap sheet on Fat Wa Loo for me?"

She frowned. The stuff I was asking was, largely, public record, but she was bucking a stack of procedures and policies going after it directly. Usually, I would have had to file a request for records, and I might have had to wait for several days to get a response.

She waited for the computer to respond, and then she let out a long, low whistle.

"You say this kid Chong beat up Fat Wa Loo?"

"Kicked the crap out of him from what I heard. Beat him with a stick."

"Maybe he should have gone ahead and killed him. Loo is a bad guy."

"Lemme see," I said, crossing around to her side of the desk.

I leaned in and caught a whiff of her perfume. I couldn't tell for certain, but I thought maybe she leaned back against me at the same time.

Eamon, you old dog, you still had it.

The computer screen detailed a list of crimes dating back almost eight years. Loo had been in court no less than twenty-eight times; almost all of them were assault charges, most of those aggravated, which meant he used some instrument. There were two manslaughter beefs, both dismissed. The rest were simple possession counts, closed by admission and paying a fine.

Gawd, I love California.

"Can you print this out for me?" I asked.

"Sure."

She tapped a couple of keys, and the inkjet printer next to the computer started to clack and whirr.

"Try to get them on the fifty-yard line," she said, handing the printout to me. "And you also owe me a crab sandwich and a couple of beers."

"As long as you don't get the idea I'm trying to ply you with spirits," I said, heading for the door.

"Oh, ply me, ply me."

"I'll call you midweek, after I get the tickets," I said, before walking out the door.

Loo was a pretty popular name in Chinatown. Still, running into it twice in one day made me curious. After hailing a cab, I pulled out my cell phone and dialed Sung Moving.

"Hello...Sung Moving," said the oft-pierced secretary. I got the impression from her pause that she had to stop for a moment to recall where she was.

"Hey, this is Mr. Gold. I came by earlier to day."

"In what did this visit regard, Mr. Cole?"

Damn. Loquacious too.

"It's Gold. G-O-L-D," I said, before regretting it. Spelling things out wasn't going to make it any easier for her. Just more things to clog her head.

"Mr. Goooollllldddd," she said, stretching it out to let me know that, by George, she got it.

"You were telling me about your manager, Chuck Loo,"

"I'm sorry, Mr. Goooollllldddd. Mr. Loo isn't in. He hasn't been here since the first of last week."

"Yes, I know. Could you tell me what his full name is, please?"

"Ummm, I guess. I have to check the files."

I began to worry. If it took her half as long to riffle through the files as it did for her to comprehend basic social intercourse, my cell phone battery would die before she got back.

Surprisingly, it only took a couple of moments.

"Mr. Gold?" she said. I was pleased that she had stopped chiding me.

"Yes."

"Mr. Loo's full name is Fat Wa Loo."

I didn't bother telling her that her manager was actually, in that case, Mr. Fat. She probably wouldn't have quit giggling for days.

Besides, I was a little preoccupied with all the synchronicity in my life over the last twenty-four hours.

"One more thing," I said. "Could you tell me if Mr... um, Loo has been hospitalized at all in the last couple of months?"

"Oh, my goodness, has he? He spent a week at General about six weeks ago. He got into a horrible fight over on Kearney."

"That's all I need to know, dear," I stopped myself and, recalling something Mr. Sung had said, I asked, "By the way, do you know where Mr Loo is?"

"No, he didn't leave word with me."

"Is it possible he's on a moving run?"

"Not in one of our trucks. They're all accounted for. In fact, we only have one out on the road right now. That's the one Sammy Chin and Lanny Gow are driving. They're in Tahoe. Should be back in a couple of days."

Superfluous information, but I wrote it down anyway.

You never know.

I thanked her and turned off the phone.

Now, wasn't that cozy? I try to find Buddy Wei for his sister, and wind up running up against the guy that one of Taylor Chu's clients, Chong Li Kow, beat to a pulp, and whom Taylor was supposed to represent in court the day after he was kidnapped. Then, Chong is represented by Louis Gai, a man known to be in the back pocket of the Sung tong. Then, it turns out that Loo manages one of Sung Chow Li's businesses, and Sung made a point of having me transported to his office to assure me that he had nothing to do with the kidnapping. That would imply that Mr. Sung had already considered the possibility that Taylor would have made the same connection.

In the way that these things do, one question leading to another, the next issue became instantly clear.

What had become of Chong Kow since the court hearing?

It was becoming difficult to figure out whom I should charge for what, the way these cases were intertwining. Might be best overall to lump them all together and split them right down the middle.

Besides, as I had already noted to Shirley Jones, I was bucks up before sending out the first bill.

SIX

I laid it all out for Taylor Chu while I glued up a couple of sheets of three-quarter inch birch plywood to bandsaw into an outside mold for a Kasha-style guitar I was planning to build someday.

"Strange," he said, sipping from a bottle of the Anchor Steam Beer I had picked up on the way to Montara.

"Yep."

"You think I ought to call Sung? You know, talk to him personally?"

"I wouldn't chance it, at least not yet. Sung may have been fishing, telling me we both knew you were still alive. That doesn't seem to be general knowledge on the street."

"But, if he kidnapped me and then let me go, why would he be sending me a message now?"

"Throw you off the track. We don't know why you were snatched yet. Maybe it was all a big mistake. Some pinhead street soldier misinterpreted a directive from Sung and decided to put the bag on you. Hell, I don't know, Taylor. I'm still piecing it together. You can't hit what you can't see."

"What now?"

"Well, let's start by you telling me everything you know about Chong Kow."

"There's not much to tell. He recently moved to the city from DC."

"Why'd he come here? Why not LA or New York?"

"He said something about getting work here."

"Did he say where?"

"We didn't get that far. Like I said, Eamon, this was just a first appearance. I didn't plan on calling any witnesses or anything."

"But you said you did hope to talk him into pleading to simple."

"Right."

"Which was what Louis Gai actually wound up doing."

"So you said."

I finished clamping the boards together, after waiting for the aliphatic resin glue to set a bit, then set the whole mess aside to dry. While I chewed on the whole scenario, I walked into the kitchen and grabbed another bottle of the Anchor Steam.

"Okay, did you talk with Chong about pleading out?"

"No, not as I recall. I interviewed him once, in the holding cell behind the courtroom. I had just been assigned the case from the bench, and I wanted to at least lay eyes on my client before standing up with him."

"Hmmmm."

"What are you thinking, Eamon?"

"You do a lot of work for the tongs, Taylor?"

"You know better than that. Once in a while I get a guy who's really connected, but I don't take money directly from any of the families."

"But Louis Gai is practically a tong *consigliere*, or whatever the Chinese word is."

"I wouldn't go that far..."

"But it's substantially true, right?"

"He does a lot of court work for tong members, yes."

"So, one might ask, how did he get assigned to Chong Kow's case so soon after you were nabbed?"

I let that one sink in for a moment. Finally Taylor nodded.

"Someone wanted Gai handling the case."

"Someone who didn't know you were already planning to get the kid on the sidewalk the next day."

"Yeah. Someone who really wanted Chong on the sidewalk."

"Because there was something he was supposed to do. Jesus, it's nice to talk with someone who hasn't lost the capacity for reason, Taylor. This is the way I see it. Chong was locked up at a tremendously inopportune time for someone, probably one of the tong Dragon Heads. He had a job to do, and this someone needed him on the streets. They didn't know you were going to talk him into copping, and there was no easy way to get you taken off the case, since you'd been put on it by the judge. They had to get you out of the way for a couple of days, long enough for Chong to do what he was supposed to do, without you asking a lot of questions about his whereabouts. What do you want to bet that Chong Kow is already back in DC?"

"I don't like your inference, Eamon."

"Why would someone come all the way across the country to do a job for one of the Dragon Heads?"

"This is getting scary."

"You know what these guys use out-of-town talent for, don't you?"

"I've heard."

"So, you disappear, Chong gets sprung from the lockup, and then you're released three days later, after a body with your license in its back pocket washes up on the City side of the bay."

"Two birds with one stone."

"Bingo. Whoever owned that body was Chong's intended target. The license in the pocket was a message to you not to dig too deeply, or the next time the license could be in *your* pocket."

We both sat and took long draws from the bottles of beer.

"Jesus," Taylor said, almost a prolonged whisper.

"They really wanted to stick it to this guy, the one they chucked off the bridge."

"What do you mean?"

"What's the worst thing you can say to a fella down in Chinatown? Worse than 'fuck your mother?'"

"*Sok nika tow.* Cut off your head."

"Damn straight. They didn't decapitate this dude just to make everyone think he was you. That was just the gravy. They wanted to put the curse on him in addition to killing him. He must have done something really bad."

"What are you going to do?" he asked.

"Good question. My first impulse is to find out where Chong Kow is now. Like I said, if he's a hired talent, he's probably back in DC already, if he was really from there to begin with. For all we know, he lied to you about that. Could be he's from Hong Kong."

"Hong Kong?"

"The tongs are like branch offices for the Triads in Hong Kong. The tongs act like a benevolent organization or chamber of commerce for the businesses in Chinatown, but they pay a heavy percentage of their cut back to the Triads. So, if you really want to get rid of someone, all the best talent comes from over there."

"And this looks like it was a big job."

"It's not every day they impart the supreme insult."

"You think you can find Chong?"

"I don't know," I said. "I can try. That's not my real problem, though. We still don't know which of the Dragon Heads had you kidnapped. The more I think about it, the less I like Sung for that one. Why would Chong show up to work for Sung, and then beat the bejeezus out of one of Sung's prime street managers? And, there's something else."

"What's that?"

"What do you have on Sung? Why's he so scared of you?"

"I don't know what you mean."

"He went to a lot of trouble to get a message to you, that you shouldn't hold him responsible for what happened to you. That means he was afraid you might try. What is it you're holding back?"

"I wish I knew," he said.

———

I got back to the office around five-thirty. This time I took a moment to clip the Browning to my belt before traipsing up the stairs. As soon as I hit the downstairs door, I was glad I had. At the top of the stairs, my door was open.

At first I was alarmed, but then I realized that Chan had never closed the door before hustling me off to see Sung Chow Li. I walked up the stairs and directly to my answering machine next to the window facing out on the Golden Gate.

"'Bout time you showed up," someone said from the other side of the room.

I tried not to jump, but it was pretty much a lost cause.

"Gotcha," Frank Raymond said.

"How long have you been here?" I asked.

"About two jiggers," he said, pointing at the bottle of Glenlivet. "I seem to recall asking you to steer clear of the Chu investigation."

"I seem to recall saying I'd keep an eye out for you. Haven't seen you all day."

"You've seen a bunch of other people though, including Sung."

"You got a tail on me, Frank?"

"What do you think? I can't stay long, so I just want you to answer one question."

"That'll be the day. What do you want to know?"

"Where's Taylor Chu?"

I grabbed a glass from the rolltop desk I use as a bar and took the bottle of Glenlivet from him. He'd had more than two jiggers, unless Chan had helped himself to my stash before taking me to see Sung.

"Tough question. Have you tried the morgue?"

"Don't bullshit me. We both know that body that got pulled from the bay wasn't Chu."

"Do we, now?"

"Coroner caught that one in about fifteen minutes. You know there are about twenty ways to estimate the age on a person? Growth plates in the forearm, coronary condition, degree of osteoarthritis in the spine. Doc figures the guy we pulled from under the Bay Bridge was no more than twenty-five. Chu is pushing forty. You have Chu holed up somewhere?"

"Would that be a crime?"

"He's a material witness. It would amount to obstruction."

"You gonna run me in, Frank? Because that would ruin my plans for the evening. I work for attorneys and bail bondsmen. They'd have me out in about an hour, but I'd still be late for dinner with Heidi downstairs."

"You wanna answer my question?"

"You want to quit busting my balls? You give me a minute, and I can tell you some things you might want to know. You keep playing tough, and I might just let you take me in just to watch you do the paperwork."

He gave me the stare again, that worn-out cop gawp that spoke volumes about how poorly he regarded the way I'd managed my life over the last ten years.

Screw him if he can't take a joke.

"Hand me the bottle," he said, finally.

I pushed it across the desk toward him. He poured about half an inch in his glass and set the bottle back down on the fake walnut.

"Okay, what do you know?"

"First, let's say you're right, and Taylor Chu is alive. Have you stopped to wonder how his license might have turned up in the back pocket of a headless corpse in the west bay?"

"Jeez, you know, I never thought about that. Why don't you enlighten me?"

"Someone would have to take it off of him, of course. Now, Chu hasn't shown up for almost a week. That means that when *whoever* lifted his license, they took him with it, right?"

"It's a possibility."

"So, let's follow up on that possibility for a moment. Let's say that *whoever* snatched him decided they didn't want him anymore. Put yourself in Chu's place. How would you feel if you were walking down, say, California Street, and saw the local paper claim you as dead?"

"Go on."

"I can think of a dozen reasons at that point why you might not want to show your face. Bunches of questions that need answers. You might decide that it's a good idea to lie low for awhile, until you can assure yourself it's safe to raise your head."

"Poor choice of words."

"Call it irony. You following me so far?"

"Like a Rand and McNally."

"Good. This is the part where I give you a tip. There are three guys out there. Names are Buddy Wei, Chuck Loo, and Chong Kow. All of them are missing. Two of them are still breathing. You find them, and I'll bet the other one will be the dude you found tossed off the bridge. One of the two who can still talk will be the one who killed him."

"And the third?"

"I haven't figured out how he fits in yet."

Frank pulled out his notebook and a pen.

"Those names again?"

———————

I told Frank everything except where I had Chu stashed. Some of it I gave him as hypotheticals, because I felt safer that way.

He left about six-thirty. I still had an hour and a half before Heidi planned to close the gallery, so I walked up to the Wharf and bought a takeout bucket of steamed oysters and a couple of Buds to pass the time. I really wanted the oysters raw, but after about age forty I found that they didn't agree with me anymore.

While I ate, I tried to place a call to Wei Ma Lo. I got a machine, and I left a message for her to call me. I had used up a little more than half her retainer over the course of the day, and she had a right to know what she had bought. For the time being, that wasn't a whole hell of a lot.

I used the remote control to turn on the stereo, tuned it to a jazz station, and spun my seat around to watch the bay out the back window. There was no fog, so I could see the lights of the waterfront restaurants out in Sausalito, and the parade of traffic crossing the Golden Gate toward Mount Tam and Muir Beach. It was a picture postcard, a view millions of people would have died for, and all I could think about was the mess Taylor Chu had wrought in my already untidy life.

SEVEN

The late hours and Heidi's overactive libido must have finally caught up with me, because I slept through the night at her place. I woke up the next morning in an empty bed, with a searing bright light pouring in through the window. Somewhere, through the fog of trying to wake up, I heard the steady white noise of a shower.

Minutes later, Heidi pranced in, all two yards of her naked buxom self dripping from the shower.

"You want to borrow a couple of towels the next time you come over?" I asked.

"Feels good to air dry," she said. "Reminds me of the beach where I grew up."

"Where was that?"

"Germany. My father was in the military. It's an old story. He got stationed there, and my mother saw an opportunity to grab off a piece of the American dream."

"Boy, when you get nostalgic, it's a three-hanky affair."

"You didn't know my mother. She was eight kinds of conniving. I was lucky to survive that childhood. You have work to do today?"

"A couple of things."

"Thought you were - how'd you say it? - bucked up?"

"Bucks up. Yeah. I am. You know what they say, though. You can never be too rich or... Jeez, what is it they say, anyway?"

"Too rich or too thin."

"Yeah. Well, since I can forget about the thin part, I figure I need to do a little work. I saw you got the new paintings in yesterday."

"Sold two right off the bat."

"Class will out."

"You want breakfast?"

We ate in her kitchen. She scrambled up some eggs, about a half dozen, and several pieces of toast. We sat at her kitchen table and ate and drank coffee and talked about almost everything except Taylor Chu, which was still a taboo topic. It was downright domestic.

Finally, she proclaimed it time to get ready to open the gallery. I showered while she dressed, and then I drove her down to the Hyde Street Pier. Rather than go up to my office, I drove over to the Russian Hill house to get a change of clothes and check my mail.

Having learned from experience, I stowed the Browning in my belt before I closed the garage door and walked up the steps of the house. As other experience had taught me, when I had the damned thing I didn't need it. The house was quiet and empty.

I considered that two of its best features.

An hour later, shaved, showered, and smelling like an aftershave factory, I climbed back into the car, stashed the Browning in the glove compartment, so I might actually run across a clue or something, and drove over to the *Chronicle* building.

Kevin Krantz was one of my few friends in junior high school, at a time when my growth spurt was about fifteen months ahead of any other kid in school, and his face looked like he washed it with a chainsaw. We had both worked on the school newspaper, thereby somehow solidifying our status as first-class geeks. He wrote the torrid personals column, full of real and imagined pairings like *What's up with Stokes and Steph?*. I took pictures of the sports teams. He still writes for a paper. I still take pictures from time to time, but not many of them get published.

Kevin had gone on to Phi Beta Kappa at USC, where he got a journalism degree. I later graduated from taking pictures of football players to becoming one, before I blew out my knee, playing wide receiver for San Francisco State. We had remained friends, though, even after our lives took dramatically different paths. Kevin now edits the business section of the *Chronicle*.

He was sitting at his desk, perusing the *Wall Street Journal*, when I popped into his office and dropped into one of his chairs. He never looked up from the paper.

"Hey, Eamon," he said.

"Kevin."

"How's that Genutech stock working out for you?"

Kevin had given me a tip to buy Genutech about six months earlier, just before they came out with that week's newest, fastest processor. I had ignored him. Ignoring him had been a bad idea.

"It's working out great for someone, Kev. Me, I just figured it would disrupt my balanced, acetic lifestyle."

"Want another tip?"

"Desperately."

He put down the *Journal* and grabbed a piece of scrap paper, on which he wrote a single word. He handed it to me across the desk.

"How many shares do you suggest?" I asked.

"How many can you afford?"

I folded the paper and stuck it in my jacket pocket.

"Thanks, Kevin."

"Bullshit. You're no more likely to buy that stock than you were to buy Genutech."

"You never know. How's Ginnie?"

About a year earlier, Kevin's wife, Ginnie, had been enjoying a nice hot shower when she ran across this funny knot in her left breast.

It had been a long year.

"The doctor wants to try stem cell therapy, since the chemo tanked out."

I nodded, as if I really understood what stem cell therapy was.

"It's just a matter of time," he said, after a long pause. "We'll keep fighting, but it's beginning to look a lot like Ginnie and I are Sam Houston and Davy Crockett, and the goober is Santa Ana."

"That's tough," I said, really meaning it. "Think she'd like me to drop by, spend a little time with her?"

"If you have time. She likes you. Somehow, you cheer her up. So, how are you doing?"

"Better than you, apparently."

I could talk to Kevin like this. Not many people can, but I can.

"Most likely. You need something?"

"Just some background stuff. You know anything about a guy named Barney Gates?"

"The restaurateur from Richmond? Sure."

"What's he up to?"

"Pretty low profile. Net worth is around twenty mil. He has seven restaurants up and running in five cities. Word has it he's working on doing something in the city."

"Sherman Fong?"

"I hadn't heard that, but thanks for the tip. So, Gates and Fong are partnering..."

"Is that significant?"

"Could be. There's a lot of money under that roof."

"Still and all, it's just a restaurant."

"Yeah, and Planet Hollywood was just a restaurant. Hard Rock Café. I could go on and on. The right idea at the right time can take off like Harry Potter. I'll look into it."

"Any history with Gates that might indicate some shady activities?" I asked. "Is there any sign of mob ties, anything like that?"

"Not on the surface. Why? What have you heard?"

"Nothing, really. His name came up while I was investigating something else, and I just want to be thorough."

Kevin didn't say anything, but he just kept looking at me over his glasses.

"Serious," I said, crossing my heart.

"Whatever."

"What about Sherman Fong?"

"You mean, besides the fact that he's all tonged up? That's the story with just about every businessman in Chinatown."

"Is there anything special about his ties with the Triads?"

"Nothing special. He pays his protection cut, just like everyone else. I haven't heard any talk indicating that he's in with the gang structure or anything. No, Eamon, both of them are just doing business. Maybe they fudge on the taxes, maybe they run it a little close on Fair Labor Standards Act stuff, but overall they're both pretty clean."

I started to get up.

"That's what I figured. I needed to check it out, though."

"I understand. You seeing anyone right now?"

"There's this woman who runs the gallery underneath my office, but it's not serious."

"Well, serious or not, maybe you'd like to get together sometime? Maybe drive across to Oakland, eat at Bridges or something?"

The message was clear. Ginnie was short-time, and Kevin wanted to make what was left as normal as possible.

"You bet," I said. "I'll talk with Heidi about it later today."

"You do yourself a favor," he said as I started out the door. "You find some disposable cash, and you put it into that stock I gave you. You won't regret it."

I thanked him again and walked down to the parking garage to retrieve my car.

As I headed south, I punched in the number to my Montara house on the cell phone. Taylor Chu answered on the third ring.

"How's the icebox looking?" I asked.

"You're short on beer. I could use some colas, maybe some fresh corned beef and a loaf of bread. Think there's any chance you might bring some vegetables by?"

"I'm making a mental list," I said. "I'll be there in about an hour."

I stopped off at the Safeway in Pacifica and dropped about fifty of Sung Chow Li's dollars on provisions. I picked up a couple of bags of salad, some tomatoes and cucumbers, a pound or two of fresh-sliced corned beef, and some rye bread. The beer and the colas were the most expensive things I bought. By my tally, the beer cost about three times as much per gallon as gasoline, but you never saw anyone bitching about that on television.

I picked up the tail as I drove up the hill on the PCH heading out of Pacifica. It was a late model Pontiac, and I wouldn't have noticed it at all if it hadn't managed to get a bird smashed into the front grill. I had seen the car behind me as I drove through the ugly neighborhoods in Daly City, but I hadn't thought anything about it at the time except that, sooner or later, that dead bird was going to start to stink something awful.

Now, after I had spent a half hour in the market, the Dead Pigeon Pontiac was still behind me. I considered calling Chu, but thought better of it. There are all kinds of sophisticated electronic gadgets out there, and I already knew that a good wide-band hand-held radio scanner could pick up the cellular conversation in less than a minute.

I picked up the pace as I drove down the hill toward the Chart House in Montara, and was doing about fifty-five as I blew right by the street leading up to my house there.

The tail was doing a pretty sloppy job of it, even discounting the serendipitous deceased bird in the grille. When I sped up, he sped up. When I slowed, he slowed. That told me stuff.

A good tail is a three-car job, preferably with none of them carrying decomposing fauna in the bodywork. If this guy had thought about it, he might have passed me when I slowed down, keeping in mind that he could watch where I went as easily in the rear-view mirror as he could out the windshield. This guy, though, just kept himself planted a hundred feet behind my bumper. That meant he might be alone, for one thing, and relatively stupid for another.

I reached over and unlatched the glove compartment, just in case I needed the Browning. The best-case scenario was that he was just following me to see where I went. On the other hand, if he intended anything more sinister, I wanted to be prepared.

Outside Half Moon Bay, I picked up the second car in the tail. So much for my single-car theory. A guy in a Dodge coupe pulled out ahead of me just before Bonny Doon beach. I might have missed him, but he kept looking up into the rear-view mirror, right after he passed every road. He was watching for me to turn off.

I was so intent on the Dodge in front of me, I didn't notice when the Pontiac pulled off. That meant I'd be seeing another car behind me shortly. I jotted down the license number of the car in front and waited for it to slow and turn.

Sure enough, just past Half Moon Bay, a third car turned in behind me two streets before the car in front veered off to the left.

The new car was a Mercedes. I decided to make it interesting, so I pulled my car off the road onto the left shoulder at the next scenic overlook. The Mercedes drove on by, but one of the two fellows in the front seat stared directly at me as they passed.

I puckered up and blew him a kiss.

The next place the Mercedes could turn off was almost half a mile ahead, so I whipped my car around in the overlook to head back north, and turned down the same road the Dodge in front of me had taken.

I did a quick u-turn and waited just far enough back from the stop sign so that the Mercedes couldn't see me there.

A minute later, the Mercedes drove by, heading north.

I pulled out and started following it, taking a moment to write down the license number. Five minutes later, I looked back, and there was the Pontiac. I almost missed it, because the pigeon had been removed from the front bumper. Apparently Car Number Two had advised him that he was being a little too obvious. That meant they were communicating, which wasn't much of a surprise, but it was nice to know.

The only license number I didn't have was the Pontiac. It has been my experience that the things I didn't know had a tendency to jump up and bite me in the ass. The Pontiac only had one guy, the driver, in it, and I already knew he wasn't very bright, so I decided to get to know him a little better.

As we neared the top of the hill between Montara and Pacifica, there was a gated road bearing off to the left. I saw through the windshield of the Mercedes that there was a long procession of cars following a truck and trailer carrying a backhoe trudging up the hill in the other direction, so I figured it would give us some time.

I veered off to the left, onto the turnoff leading to the gated road. As I expected, the Pontiac followed me. As soon as the tractor-trailer reached the top of the hill, I slammed on the brakes, shifted into park, and grabbed the Browning. I was out the car door before the Pontiac even came to a stop behind me.

The long line of cars following the backhoe would keep anyone from bothering us for a few moments. I walked up to the Pontiac and rapped the glass with the barrel of the Browning.

The driver couldn't have been more than eighteen, and like an idiot he actually rolled down the window. That wasn't such a bad idea, since my next move would have been to break the glass and pull him through it. I stuck the Browning into his left ear.

"You wanted to talk?" I asked.

He was Asian, which so far this week had meant Chinese. He just stared ahead, breathing hard. I was pissing him off. I didn't care.

"Are you with Sung Chow Li?" I asked.

He didn't answer, but he blinked a lot when I mentioned the tong boss.

"Who are your buddies?"

Nothing.

This was getting old, and any minute I was going to have company. I opened the door and pulled the kid out of the Pontiac.

"C'mon," I said. "Let's take a ride."

I pushed him toward my car and made him get in on the driver's side and slide across the seat. I sat down.

"Seatbelt," I said. "Safety first."

He ignored me. I guess he thought seatbelts were pussy.

Keeping the Browning trained on him with my left hand, I started the car and put it in drive. I pulled out into the line of cars behind the backhoe, to a chorus of horns and some tire squeals. It made sense. Somewhere up ahead on the road to Half Moon Bay was the Dodge. At the end of this very long line of cars was the Mercedes. As long as I stayed where I was, neither of them could get very close to me.

"First chance I get, I'm turning around and heading back into San Francisco," I said. "We're going to pay a little visit to Mr. Sung. If you work for him, he's going to want to know what a lousy tail you are. If you don't..."

I shrugged.

We reached the Chart House, and I dove off the road and around to the back. The tail end of the line of cars was still around a corner, so the Mercedes couldn't see me, if indeed it hadn't already stopped at the turnoff where I had left the Pontiac.

A moment later, I saw the Dodge busting ass north on Highway 1. Apparently they'd gotten the word that Car Number One was out of action. I waited a couple of minutes, and then started driving north myself. Several minutes later, I hit a side road that I knew led to the interstate. I hoped Cars Two and Three didn't know about it.

I looked over at the kid, and I could swear he was about to cry.

"Maybe we won't go see Mr. Sung after all," I said.

He started to turn his head in my direction, but stopped himself.

"I have the license numbers of the other two cars, the Dodge and the Mercedes. I can find out who owns them, real easily. I could just take those names to Mr. Sung. I don't need your scrawny ass."

I thought I saw him stiffen a little.

"Lots of empty space out here, isn't there?" I asked. "Earthquake gullies, creeks. Lots of places I could dump you where you wouldn't be found for days. What do you think, kid? Maybe we ought to take a quick detour?"

He really was crying now, but he was holding back the sobs. I figured he hadn't been in the States for more than a year. Maybe he'd seen a bunch of bootleg American gangster films over in China, knew what it meant to *take a ride*. He probably thought I was going to walk him out in the woods somewhere and give him a dose of the nine-millimeter migraine.

That suited me just fine. I could use an attitude like that.

"Let's try this again," I said. "Let's start with your name."

"Wu Dong," he snuffled.

"Okay, Wu Dong, what's your street name?"

"Frankie."

"Good. I'm Eamon. No street name. Just Eamon."

He didn't say anything, just sniffed a couple of times.

"Does your mother know you're running tails for the tong?" I asked.

"She don't know what I do."

"I figured as much. So, Frankie, what's going to happen when I walk you into Mr. Sung's office? They going to welcome you with open arms?"

Silence.

"Maybe you don't even work for Mr. Sung."

More silence.

"Whatever," I said, as I turned off the road onto a dirt lane leading off into a farm. "You look around, see if there's a particularly nice spot where you want to rot for the next couple of days."

"Not with Sung Chow Li," he said.

There was a hint of desperation in his voice. In his place, there probably would have been a little of it in mine, too.

"Which one, then?"

"Hop Sing tong."

The Hop Sing was one of the oldest tongs in the city. There were records of it dating all the way back to the Barbary Coast days. The Hop Sing tong had been a major player in the Opium Wars, both in Hong Kong and stateside. Hop Sing snakeheads controlled much of the person smuggling out of Shanghai.

This kid was well-connected.

I stopped the car, raising clouds of fine dust in billows around the doors. I turned toward Frankie Wu and rammed the barrel of the Browning just as far up his nose as I thought hygienically sound. He whimpered a little.

"Why were you following me?"

More whimpers.

I was taking a chance of overworking this ploy. Some guys, you cram a gun up their nose, they turn to jello and crap their pants, and that's the end of the conversation. I was hoping Frankie was made of tougher stuff.

I pulled back the hammer of the Browning. Just to be a little safe in a dangerous situation, I took my finger off the trigger and laid it on the handle of the gun. I didn't want any accidents. I had just had the car cleaned.

"One more chance," I said. "Why were you following me?"

"We were looking for Taylor Chu!" he wailed.

"You thought I might lead you to him?"

"Yes!"

"Taylor Chu's dead, chum. Haven't you read the papers?"

"No he isn't. Everyone knows he's alive."

"So who was it that got tossed off the Bay Bridge?"

Frankie shook his head. I couldn't tell whether that meant he didn't know or wouldn't say.

"What interest does the Hop Sing tong have in finding Chu?"

"I don't know."

"Is there a contract out on him? Were you guys planning on zagging him?"

Frankie shook his head again.

"What's that mean? No contract?"

"I don't know. We were just supposed to find him."

"And you figured I might know where he is."

Frankie nodded.

"Get out of the car, Frankie."

He tried to turn to look at me, but the gun barrel up his schnozz made that inconvenient.

"What are you going to do?" he asked.

"One thing at a time. Get out of the car."

He opened the passenger side door and stepped out. As he did, I climbed out behind him, just in case he thought about doing something stupid, like running.

I looked around, sniffed the air. There was a light breeze, but no sounds of auto traffic.

"On the ground," I ordered. "Face down."

He was shaking like a chihuahua, but he dropped to his knees, and lowered himself until he was lying in the dirt on his stomach.

"Let me give you some advice," I said, leveling the Browning and pointing it at the back of his head. "For what it's worth, that is. If you want to play dangerous games, you have to be prepared to lose."

I jerked the pistol an inch to the right and blew a nine-millimeter round into the dirt next to his ear. It cratered the dry earth and threw dust and pebbles into his hair. He screamed, but he didn't jump up. There was a sudden sour smell in the air. A wet brown stain began to spread across the back of his jeans. The side of his face was pockmarked with black and gray cordite blowback.

"No next time. Right, Frankie?" I said.

He shook his head.

"No next time," he said, sobbing.

"You can make your way back to the city?"

He nodded, his nose rubbing in the dirt.

"I'm going to climb back into my car. I don't want to see you stand up. You understand?"

He nodded again.

"I understand."

"Good. When I drive off, you just count to one hundred, real slowly, and then you can get up. Your car is about ten miles back, if your buddies left it there. If not, improvise."

I didn't wait for him to answer.

EIGHT

I hit the interstate and drove back into San Francisco. Near Candlestick, I doubled back and made my way across the hills to Highway 1, checking for tails all the way.

It was past one o'clock by the time I got back to Montara. I hadn't seen anyone that looked even remotely Chinese or suspicious, but I parked three streets back from my house just the same.

I walked in through the carport door and dropped the food on the counter.

"Taylor!" I called.

He walked in from the bedroom.

"We can do this one of two ways," I said. "Either you get straight with me right now, or I'm going to drag your lying lawyer ass straight back into San Francisco and let you talk with the police."

"What..." he started.

"Bad start, pal. I'm going to ask the questions from here on in. Just what is it you're doing for the tongs?"

"Nothing."

"Then maybe you have some explanation why the Hop Sing put a tail on me today, looking for you."

"Hop Sing?"

"So far, the Hop Sing and the Sung Chow Li are both asking after your whereabouts. That leads me to think maybe this involves more than some imported Chinese button man you were supposed to defend."

"I told you everything you wanted to know already," he protested. "You might want to take a moment and remember that I was the one who was kidnapped. They didn't tell me anything. I'm still trying to figure it out myself."

"You're involved in something bad, Taylor," I said. "I'm tired of getting it in bits and pieces. Get your stuff."

"I don't understand."

"We're taking a ride. You being dead has proven to be a huge inconvenience for me. It's time for a little resurrection."

"Where are you taking me?"

"Inspector Raymond seems a good place to start. After he's finished with you maybe we'll drop by Sung's office. By dinnertime, we might even make it by the Hop Sing territory. Someone knows what this is all about."

"No!" he said. "You can't do this."

I pulled my cell phone from my jacket pocket and started to dial Frank Raymond's private office number.

"Maybe you're right," I told him. "We'll just let them come to us."

"Wait! Damn it, Eamon, give me a minute!"

I stopped dialing.

"What is it? You act like you enjoy this being dead thing."

"It's been restful."

"Don't fuck with me. What are you hiding from?"

He didn't say anything. Instead, he turned and walked back into the bedroom.

I followed him.

"Do you know what a grass sandal is, Eamon?"

I knew, but I let him tell it his way.

"I've heard the term."

"It's the Chinese name for a sort of glorified bagman. The grass sandal acts as a go-between, shuttling back and forth between tong heads. Sometimes he carries money. Sometimes just messages. Remember your Shakespeare?"

"A little."

"The Herald in *Henry V*, the fellow who was able to ride unmolested between the French and English armies. He would be a classic version of the grass sandal. It's a big deal in the tongs to be the grass sandal. Very honorable. The grass sandal has the safest job in any gangland organization in the world. Nobody would dare to harm him. Nobody robs him. Nobody even looks at him sideways. He gets free meals at any restaurant. He walks into a clothing store and walks out in a new suit."

"I get the idea. The grass sandal is a big deal."

"There are seven tongs in Chinatown. Did you know that?"

"Yeah. Get on with it, Taylor."

"Each tong has its own grass sandal."

"Okay."

"Can you imagine what would happen to the entire structure of the tongs if anything were to happen to one of them?"

I thought about it for a moment.

"Destabilization," I said, finally.

"Exactly. The tongs have developed this delicate balance. Each one runs its own program. Nobody interferes with anyone else's business. Sure, every once in a while some street manager gets a little overzealous and decides to make a try at muscling into some other manager's action, but it's always dealt with quickly and quietly. The tong Dragon Heads all know what would happen if the system were knocked on its ass."

I knew what he was talking about. There had been two major massacres in the Chinatown underworld in the last quarter century. Both of them kept the Coroner's office busy for weeks.

"Get relevant," I said. "You still haven't told me what you're hiding from."

"This kid, Chong?"

"The button man from D.C.?"

"He told me something the first day we met, in the holding cell behind the courtroom where I was assigned his case. He told me he wanted to get the trial over as quickly as possible, that he had a job to do."

"The guy they tossed off the bridge and pretended was you."

"No, Eamon. That was incidental. Chong didn't tell me much in that conversation, but I figured out pretty quickly what he was doing. I heard bits and pieces from other clients, and finally I put it all together."

"Yeah?"

"One of the Dragon Heads brought Chong over to kill one of the grass sandals."

I turned and walked to the kitchen. There were two beers left in the refrigerator. I popped the caps off both of them. When I turned back around, Taylor was there. I handed one of them to him.

"This is nuts," I said.

"That's what I thought."

"Why would a Dragon Head do something like that? It would be suicide. Remember the Golden Dragon Massacre in '77?"

"Vividly."

"The tongs took years to recover. Why would one of them want to go down that road again?"

"Maybe because he thinks this time he can win."

I sat on the stool at my workbench and looked at him.

"You'd better explain that."

"You know the tongs are the stateside agents for the Triads in Hong Kong."

"Of course. Everyone knows that."

"In 1999, Hong Kong reverted back to the Chinese Republic."

"Ancient history, Taylor."

"The Reds in Beijing have tried to corral some of the more... capitalist elements in Hong Kong and Macau, but it's been difficult. The Red Guards can be ruthless, but they aren't used to dealing with shadow organizations. Meanwhile, the Snakeheads have been smuggling folks out of China so fast that it looks like the Rapture in some villages."

"It's been in all the papers."

"You think every soul they smuggle in is just some poor schmuck who doesn't know he's letting himself in for a life of indentured service?"

I thought about it for a moment.

"One of the Triads is salting Chinatown with soldiers," I surmised.

"Seems that way."

"They're massing their forces, placing them in deep cover jobs, and waiting for an opportunity to take over. The Triads know their days in Hong Kong are numbered, and they need a new place to play."

"Greener grass."

"So, what are you saying? One of the tongs is ready now to set off World War Three in Chinatown?"

"The best way to light off a range war on Grant Avenue is to kill a grass sandal. One of the Dragon Heads has gone to a lot of trouble to set this up."

"Which one?"

He shrugged.

"If I knew that," he said, "I wouldn't be so scared."

I chugged the beer, and immediately went to the kitchen, where I opened one of the beers I had bought at the market in Pacifica. It was warmish. I didn't really care.

I walked back into the living room and sat at my workbench. Most times, I would have grabbed a piece of instrument-in-progress and started working on it to clear my head, but that wasn't going to happen this time. Taylor retreated to the kitchen, where I could hear him putting the groceries away.

"Do I get to stay here for a while?" he asked from the other room.

"I can't just sit on this, you know."

"I figured."

"You also figured that, sooner or later, you'd dump this in my lap and I'd have to run with it."

"Um hmmm."

"That's pretty devious, you know."

He walked back into the living room, with a warm beer of his own, and sat on the couch.

He smiled.

"I'm a lawyer, Eamon."

———

We decided to keep Taylor Chu dead for another day. That would give me time to bird-dog this grass sandal story a little, and maybe get tailed again. I made a unilateral decision of my own, to keep the Browning clipped to my belt every waking moment, and under my pillow when I slept. The tongs had a reasonably decent history of keeping their internecine squabbles among themselves. Someone, though, was apparently determined to break tradition. I didn't want to get caught in the crossfire without a little muscle of my own to flex.

I left the Montara house a couple of hours later. I still had some errands to run.

As I drove through Daly City, I punched Wei Ma Lo's telephone number on the cell phone again, trying to give her an update on her brother Buddy. The line was busy, which I decided was better than getting a machine.

I drove into the city and parked at a surprisingly available spot on Columbus. I walked down Green Street toward the bay and the North Beach smell of garlic and red, ripe tomatoes. In the distance, a couple of blocks up, I could make out the Whiskey-A-Go-Go and a bunch of other strip bars. That wasn't my destination, though.

I turned left on Montgomery Street and started the long uphill trudge toward Benny Horowitz's house. Benny and I had grown up in the same neighborhood, gotten *bar mitzvahed* the same month, but had never had much of a relationship until the last five years or so. By day, Benny was an accountant at Bank of America. In his spare time, though, he collected things. Most collectors buy stuff they find valuable and hold on to them for years. Benny collected stuff he could unload quickly, for the right price.

I rang Benny's doorbell, which was attached to a door made of the kind of Oregon myrtle I would have loved to make into about fifteen guitars. I wondered how much Benny would take for his front door. I wondered about this for maybe five minutes, until it became apparent that Benny hadn't gotten home from work yet.

I hadn't had lunch, and it had been a long stressful time since eggs and toast in Heidi's breakfast nook, so I decided to grab a bite. I walked the rest of the way to the top of the hill on Montgomery and hung a left. About a block ahead of me was a small Italian place I had tried a month or so earlier.

I ordered mussels marinara on a plate of cappellini and a glass of cheap Chianti. I was sitting by the window, munching on a piece of garlic bread, when Benny walked by.

I rapped on the window.

He stopped, squinted through the glass, and then beamed as he waved at me. Then he opened the front door and walked over to my table.

"Eamon! Long time!"

"Have a seat, Benny."

"You buying?"

"If you won't tell my mom I'm eating shellfish."

"Damn stuff will kill you. Says so in the Torah," he said, as the waitress appeared at the side of the table.

"I'll have some of what he's having," he told her, "But none of that cheap rotgut. Bring us a bottle of the...." he perused the wine list, and made a sour face, "...well, I guess this will have to do."

He pointed out the vintage he wanted, and she wrote it down and disappeared.

"Hell, they'll probably just pour it out of a jug of Carlo Rossi anyway," he said, shrugging.

"I was just at your place," I told him.

"Yeah? Sorry I missed you. I decided to hoof it home this afternoon. Good for the heart."

"You want to sell your front door?"

"So you can butcher it up and make ukuleles out of it? No deal. What can I do for you?"

"I need some tickets to the 49ers game this Sunday."

He didn't even blink.

"How many?"

"Two, lower section, fifty-yard line."

The waitress returned with a decanted bottle of wine. Benny waved her off.

"Now go back and bring one that has the cork in it, sweetheart," he said.

She pouted, and he reached around and popped her bottom.

"Mr. Horowitz!" she yelped.

"Yeah, that's not what you called me last Saturday night. Now go get that wine, and no games this time."

She walked away, her cheeks flaming up. Maybe all four of them.

"You and the waitress?" I said.

"What can I say? I just live around the corner. I eat here a lot. You eat somewhere a few times, you get to know the staff."

"So you decided to introduce her to your staff."

He shook his head.

"I never kiss and tell, my friend. Fifty-yard line? Geez, that's a tall order. Gonna set you back."

"How much?"

"Four bills. Five if you want a parking pass."

At this rate, I was going to run through Sung Chow Li's bonus payment before dinner was over.

"Three fifty, with the pass."

"Four, and I'll throw in the pass because I like you."

"Three seventy-five, with the pass, because I can still beat you up."

We settled on three-eighty, which was a mulligan I threw him because, after all, I had no idea where else I might get the tickets, and I had promised Shirley Jones.

The waitress brought a corked bottle of wine, and Benny made a big show of sniffing the cork after it was opened. A moment later, the food arrived.

Benny speared a mussel with his fork and pulled it from the shell.

"Geez, this looks like my first girlfriend. How do the goyim eat this stuff?"

"The same way we do, with butter and garlic and tomatoes," I said, popping one into my mouth.

"The wine's not bad, but you oughta see what I got in my house."

"Dealing in wine, now?"

"It's the latest thing, Gold. You wouldn't believe it. Robert Parker raves about a wine, and a week later it zooms to three hundred, four hundred dollars a bottle. Sometimes more. The trick is to get hold of it before Parker distributes his review."

"Which you manage to do - how?"

"Which I manage to do by knowing people who set the type at Wine Spectator, and by knowing people who know which wineries Parker is visiting this week. I play hunches, buy a couple of cases as soon as I get word, and wait for the market to go bananas."

"What if you're wrong?"

"What's the harm? I can always drink my mistakes. Give me the money."

"Give me the tickets."

He held out his hands and flexed his fingers, in this *come on* sort of way.

I reached into my pocket and peeled four bills off the roll I had in there. He whistled lowly.

"Man, you are bucks up. If I'd known..."

I handed him the money.

"You owe me twenty," I said.

"Sure, sure. I don't have it on me, but I'll put it in the envelope when I drop the tickets off at your office tomorrow."

He wouldn't, of course, but I figured I owed him a tip.

We went in different directions when we left the restaurant. I hiked back down the hill to Columbus. There was a parking ticket stuck under my windshield wiper. I almost missed it because it was blocked by the tough-looking Chinese guy sitting on my hood.

I started to walk right past him, maybe keep on walking until I got to Mexico, but that didn't seem practical, and I needed my wheels. So, I walked just a little bit past him, to the driver's side door.

"Get off the car, Chief," I said, as I stuck the key in the lock.

He didn't say anything. He didn't even really acknowledge that I had spoken. He pulled a small penknife from his pants pocket and made a show of cleaning some dirt from under his fingernails while he stared off at the pyramid.

"It's been a long day," I said, pulling my jacket open to let him know I was strapped. "I have just about had it with you guys. Take a walk. Hassle me tomorrow. I'm not going anywhere."

He glanced at the Browning, and went back to cleaning his fingernails.

I slammed the door. I thought I saw him jump a little, but that might have been wishful thinking. Sometimes I feel this need to see myself as threatening.

"Hey, speakee Englee?" I said. "Is there some reason you aren't getting this?"

"What if I don't get off?" he asked, in fluent English.

I know a threat when I hear one. I placed my hand on the butt of the Browning.

"You won't shoot me," he said.

Sometimes, people just do stuff that pushes you over the line. This obnoxious car-sitter hadn't done much to me, but he was about to catch the shrapnel for all the shit everyone else had dumped on me all day.

I drew the Browning, stepped in close, and pressed it into his spleen.

"You feel confident about that?" I asked. "Now get off the goddamn car, asshole!"

"That's Special Agent Asshole to you, dickweed," he said, just before two unmarked, whitebread official government cars drove up and double-parked in front of and behind my car.

"I'm going to pull out my wallet," he said, putting a snide edge on it. "Let's all be nice here, and you try not to blow my liver down into the bay, okay?"

I started to put the Browning back into my belt, but one of the other agents who climbed out of the car wrapped his hand around it and took it away from me.

The guy on my car flipped open the wallet, displaying a bright, shiny badge and an official-looking ID card. Homeland Security, Division of Immigration and Naturalization.

"Name's Hong, James Hong," he said, chuckling.

"Geez, I bet you love doing that," I said.

"Bet your ass, Mr. Gold. Now, you and I are going over to that ugly green guvvy car, and we're going to have a talk. When we're done, I'll either give you back that toy pistol of yours, or I'm going to find some reason to put you away for a few years. Any questions?"

"Nope," I said. "Though, at this point, would it be possible to just skip all the other stuff and get put away for a while? I could use the rest."

He slid off the hood of the car and took me by the arm.

"Come on. Let's talk."

The car had vinyl seats, vinyl armrests, and a vinyl headliner with about ten million tiny holes in it. I think Uncle Sugar bought it for fifteen bucks from the Chrysler Corporation. One of the cookie cutter agents sat in the front seat, juicing the accelerator every minute or so, and monitoring the air conditioning system, while Hong and I sat in the back.

"First," he said, "where is Taylor Chu?"

I stared at him. I might have, involuntarily, raised one eyebrow.

"We know he isn't at your Russian Hill house, and he isn't at your girlfriend's house, and he isn't at his house or your office. That leaves that little shitpile you keep out at the beach. Would we find him there, Mr. Gold?"

"That would be the last place I saw him," I said. "But the way things are going, I couldn't swear to anything."

"We'll check it out. Don't worry. We don't want Chu for anything right now, considering that he's natural born and all, but we might want to drop by and talk with him."

"Fine by me."

"Next order of business. About an hour ago, a cop car down just north of Half Moon Bay picked up an undocumented Chinese kid named Wu Dong walking along the side of the road. According to reports, he was filthy, had dirt and rocks in his hair, and he needed an urgent change of undershorts. Would you know anything about this?"

"Yeah," I said. "I did all that to him."

"Busy, busy, busy. Well, I imagine he will have some interesting stories to tell when he gets back to Guangzhou. Next item: what did Sung Chow Li want with you yesterday?"

"He wanted me to pass a message to Taylor Chu."

Hong stared, waiting for me to volunteer the message.

I figured I could wait, too.

I was kind of surprised when Hong didn't press the issue.

"You told Inspector Raymond to look for three young Chinese nationals," he continued.

"Yeah. Buddy Wei, Chuck Loo, and Chong Kow. Wei and Loo are locals. My guess is Chong Kow has blown town. He might be back in the DC area, but I wouldn't put money on it."

"Chong Kow is dead, Mr. Gold."

On any other day, I might have been surprised, shocked, or bewildered.

Not today.

"Okay."

"You were half right, though. He did get out of town, but only barely. His car was found just off the road south of Monterey. He was still in it. Someone used half a clip on him, apparently shot him through the driver's door, then forced the car off the road, judging by the tire marks on his front fender."

"Why are you telling me this?"

"We found a slip of paper in his pocket. On it was written the words *Xinhua Voyager*."

"This isn't relevant to me."

"As it happens, *Xinhua Voyager* is the name of a container ship moored at the shipping docks in Long Beach."

"Imagine that. Can I have my gun back now?"

"The *Xinhua Voyager* is set to cast off for Hong Kong at eleven tomorrow morning. The way we figure it, Chong was planning to catch a ride back to China on it."

I didn't say anything. Apparently, nobody cared.

"We boarded the *Xinhua Voyager* about two hours ago. Homeland Security and Customs guys are still checking it out. We did, however, also check the containers it dropped off when it docked in Long Beach last week. Would you like to know what we found in one of them?"

"No."

"Signs of human habitation."

"No kidding."

"Why do I think you're way ahead of me on this story?"

"Probably because you're telling it so badly. I get the picture, Hong. The *Xinhua Voyager* smuggled a certain number of mainland Chinese citizens into the country, some of them living in a cargo container, and they were planning to take Chong back with them. You're also going to tell me that the container the smuggled Chinese were in was destined to be delivered to a business owned by one of the tong Dragon Heads in San Francisco."

"You're getting it. Would you like to know what signs of human habitation we found in that container?"

"Sure, I got nothing else to do."

"Thirty-seven bodies."

I stared at him closely for the first time since getting into the car.

"Machine gunned," he said.

"All men," I said.

"Correct."

"No women or children."

"Not a one."

"They were armed."

"To the teeth."

"Headed for San Francisco."

"Correct again. You catch on quick, Mr. Gold."

"Which Dragon Head?" I asked.

He stared at me, and then he shook his head slowly.

"Sung Chow Li."

I nodded, suddenly tired and weary.

"Yeah," I said. "That kind of figures."

"So, you see, we were sort of intrigued when a couple of Sung's hardheads dropped by yesterday to take you to see the old boy personally."

"He wanted me to tell Taylor that he wasn't behind the kidnapping."

"Maybe he was lying."

"That had occurred to me."

"So, maybe it would be nice if you told me what you've found out, Mr. Gold. Because, right at this moment, I can't see for shit what is going on in the tongs."

"The guys in the container were being brought over to take part in some kind of insurrection in Chinatown," I said. "According to the best information I have, which might be a little flimsy, Chong Kow was imported to kill a major player in one of the tongs, thereby destabilizing the structural balance in Chinatown. This would lead to open warfare, a lot like the Golden Dragon Massacre several years ago, but this time one of the Dragon Heads was prepared."

"I see," Hong said. "The container was to be delivered to one of Sung's businesses. That would imply that he's the one trying to destabilize the structure."

"Perhaps. But what about Chong Kow? If he were taking his act on the road, it would imply that he had finished his job. Have there been any high-profile murders in Chinatown over the last couple of days?"

"None."

"So, why was he running?"

"Maybe he couldn't get the job done."

"Why not?"

"Maybe nobody could find the guy he was supposed to kill."

Something cold and loathsome settled in my chest, and started to put the squeeze on my stomach.

"That doesn't make sense," I said.

"Why not?"

"You said Chong was going to the *Xinhua Voyager* to catch a ride back to Hong Kong. The container destined for Sung Chow Li came in on the Voyager. That would imply that the two are linked. Taylor Chu was supposed to represent Chong Kow in court but was kidnapped before the hearing. Chong was represented by Louis Gai. If Sung was responsible for importing Chong, and Chong found out that Taylor was the guy he was supposed to zag, there was no reason to get Taylor out of the way. Sung Chow Li wouldn't have gone to the trouble of grabbing me and bringing me all the way down to Kearney Street just to have me tell Taylor that he didn't have him nabbed. He'd have used me to get to Taylor, and then completed the job. And there's one more thing..."

"Yes," Hong said.

"Taylor Chu isn't a high roller in the Chinatown community. He's not the grass sandal."

"What about *grass sandal?*" Hong said, suddenly perking up.

"That's what Taylor told me, that he found out Chong was supposed to kill one of the grass sandals."

"And then he disappeared."

"Right."

"Mysteriously."

"Right again."

"Ostensibly kidnapped."

"So he said."

"And his license is found three days later on that body that washed up at the base of the Bay Bridge."

"Yes."

We sat there for a several minutes, cooking it over in our heads.

"Man," Hong said, finally, "I sure hope he kissed you."

"Meaning?"

"It is just no fun to get screwed without getting kissed."

He handed my gun to me. I stowed it in my belt.

"Let's go," he said. "I think we'd better have a conversation with Mr. Chu."

NINE

Someone had painted the inside of my Montara house with Taylor Chu.

I walked in with James Hong, and I immediately knew we had just stomped all over a crime scene. There was a smell in the air. If you've ever smelled it, you won't forget it, like wet hot copper mixed with sulfur.

I grabbed Hong the moment we walked through the door and pulled him back toward the carport.

"He's dead," I told him.

"What the fuck?"

"Someone got to him, in the last three hours. Have you ever done homicide work?"

"No. I'm immigration, for Chrissake."

"Okay. We call the cops. If we go inside that house, we'll fuck up the crime scene."

I pulled out my cell phone and called the Pacifica police station. I had the number on my speed dial list, along with every other PD in the five-county area.

Ten minutes later, there were four bubbletop cruisers in front of my house. A tall, bony detective named Crymes (no shit, it really is Crymes), sauntered up to Hong and me and wiped his nose with a cloth handkerchief.

"Damn allergies. So, Gold, what's the deal? Dispatch squawked out a murder."

"I haven't seen him yet, but I know the smell, Crymes. I've been hiding Taylor Chu here for the past couple of days."

"Bullshit, Gold. I read the papers. Chu's dead."

"He is for damn sure dead," I said, "but it didn't happen until today."

I introduced Special Agent Hong, and he and Crymes shook, reluctantly. Local cops have this natural antipathy for anyone hefting a federal shield, and Crymes was no exception.

"Okay," he said, "Let's check it out. You, Hong, you stay out here. I'll take Gold with me."

"Wait a minute," Hong protested. "How come Gold goes in?"

"First, it's his house. He knows where everything is supposed to be. Second, if he did hide Taylor Chu here for the past couple of days, and Chu is dead, he can identify the body. Third, Gold used to be a cop, and he knows how to walk around a crime scene without pissing on every scrap of evidence. You, being Homeland Security, would just fuck up the whole place and ruin the case. So Gold goes in, you stay out. Any more questions?"

I tried to stifle a grin. I liked Crymes. Always had. Of course, I had also noted that he had said *Gold used to be a cop* as if he wanted to add *before he totally fucked up his life*.

He reached into his shirt pocket and pulled out a small tin of Vap-O-Rub.

"Think I'll need this?" he asked.

"Jesus, the guy's only been dead an hour or two. He probably smells better than either of us."

"Speak for yourself," he said, and opened the back door.

The kitchen looked all right, but the odor of messy death hung in the air like a warning. I pulled my jacket down over my hand and clicked the light switch.

We walked into the living room, and my stomach flipped a couple of times. The drawer to my toolbox, where I stored my sharps, was pulled out and lying on the workbench.

I am a real nut for keeping sharp tools. I hone them to a state called *scary sharp*. Some woodworker told me once that the term meant you wanted to make them so sharp that it scared you to look at them. He also said you wanted to make them that way because if you did cut yourself you'd cut deeper, but it wouldn't hurt as much.

I have a fertile imagination, and I could easily envision what some of those tools could do to flesh and muscle and bone.

The smell was stronger as we approached the bedroom, with good reason.

The healthy adult human body holds about seven pints of blood. That might not sound like much, but try dumping a gallon of milk on your kitchen floor sometime and see how long it takes to mop it up. The bedroom looked as if someone had slung about six pints on the walls, the ceiling, and across the rug.

Chu was lying on the bed. Movies don't do bludgeoning justice. If you can, imagine what a human skull would look like if it were a hen's egg, and you slapped it a couple of times with a Louisville Slugger. That's what Taylor Chu's head looked like.

Before they caved in his face, though, someone had gone to work on him with my knives. I looked wistfully at the fine *bois de rose* handles and the surgical steel blades, and I mentally kissed them goodbye. I would never get them back, now that they were murder weapons.

Likewise for my cittern neck. Whoever had killed Chu had grabbed the most likely cudgel around, a nice long piece of figured hard maple shaped roughly like a blunt hatchet—the neck I had been fashioning two days earlier—and had pounded Chu's face into pudding.

It was gruesome, but not the worst I had ever seen. Still, I felt the color rise in my face. Someone had invaded my private sanctuary and had made me look like a complete idiot by wasting my client with my own possessions.

And it was no picnic for Taylor, either.

Crymes stood at the doorway, careful not to step in any of the random pools of congealing blood, and let his eyes dart from one point to another around the room.

"Just what the hell kind of place is this, anyway?" he asked, finally.

"I actually live in the city," I said. "I keep this house in Montara to use as a workshop. Before you ask, those are my knives, and they hit him with a cittern neck I was carving."

"A *what* neck?"

"Cittern. It's a musical instrument."

He pulled back from the doorway and, as if for the first time, noticed the various instruments hanging from hooks on the walls.

"Mmm," he said, and stepped back into the bedroom.

"What do you think?" I asked.

"Weeellll," he said, taking on this folksy, Central California country drawl, "I think you have the right to remain silent..."

"What the fuck?"

"The right to an attorney..."

"Come on, Crymes."

"You want to shut up long enough for me to finish this?"

"You're arresting me?"

"No. I'm informing you of your rights, because as soon as we finish here, I'm taking you down to the station house, and we are going to have a long talk. I'll decide then whether I'm gonna arrest you."

"I wasn't even here, and I can prove it."

"That should put your mind at ease. The facts, however, are these: the deceased is in your house, killed with your possessions, and you have somehow managed to not tell anyone he was here for at least two days, during which just about anything could have happened. A lot of those knife cuts look fresh, but for all I know you've been torturing poor Mr. Chu here, and when either you got what you wanted or he wouldn't talk, you decided to do a little blunt instrument root canal."

"Crymes..."

"Are you waiving your rights, Eamon?"

"What?"

"You want to think about, maybe, consulting an attorney before you say something you'll regret later?"

I couldn't help it. I tried to stop it, but the irony of the situation overwhelmed me and I couldn't stifle a chuckle, which grew into a genuine belly laugh. Crymes looked at me as if I had lost my mind.

Maybe I had.

"What are you laughin' about, Gold?"

"Christ, man," I said, pointing into the bedroom. "That *is* my attorney!"

———

The medical examiner arrived about a half hour later. During that time, the forensic team arrived and started taking photographs. I sat on the hood of my car with James Hong and considered all the angles. They kept coming up obtuse.

Another hour passed, and the sun started to dip low on the Pacific horizon, bouncing stray beams of crystalline razor light off the placid water and into my eyes. Both Hong and I stepped into the relative gloom of the carport.

Finally, Crymes came out.

"Give me your gun, Eamon," he said.

I opened my jacket and handed over the Browning. Crymes started to escort me to his car.

"Wait a minute," I said.

He gave me this dead fish stare, like I was about to use up the last of my very few favors.

"Let me take my car," I said. "You're not going to book me tonight, and I need a way back into the city. You can let one of your uniforms drive if you like, but I'm going to need my wheels later."

Crymes and I had known one another for several years. I had handled several cases in the Half Moon Bay area, and I have a habit of letting the local detectives know when I might be traipsing around the local hotels, loitering and acting vagrantly. I had even managed to help him on a couple of his own cases, when I stumbled across information he could use.

Still, he regarded me with all the warmth most guys on the job save for ex-cops who have taken the work private. Cops, in general, make just enough money to slowly starve. When a uniform or a gold shield goes into business for himself, it often means a substantial increase in disposable income. You trade your security for it, but it can be worth the swap. A lot of guys on the force, though, don't have the balls to go it alone, without a ton of backup. They resent it when you rub their noses in your own success, whether you mean to or not. They're paranoid that way.

Despite the fact that Crymes and I were on a first-name basis, he considered me a valid, if unlikely, suspect. In this case, I was a suspect requesting access to my wheels. That ran counter to his sense of control over the situation. I was hoping he would weigh our history against his natural suspicions and decide in my favor.

"Don't presume what I'm going to do and what I'm not," he said. "Right now, I got enough stuff to keep you busy in the interview room for the next week."

I held up my hands, palms out, in what I hoped was a supplicating and beseeching manner. I also put on my most convincing Tom Sawyer grin.

"Jenks can drive you," he said, at last. "But you'll have to be cuffed."

"You'll uncuff me as soon as we get to the station?"

"Jesus, Gold."

"Just asking."

Crymes turned to one of the uniforms, a kid around twenty-five.

"Can you drive a stick?" he asked the kid, whom I presumed to be Jenks.

"Sure," Jenks said.

"Take Mr. Gold's car to the station. Let your partner drive the squad."

He turned back to me.

"You're coming with me," he said.

I shrugged. He retained control, and I had access to my ride when the grilling was over.

It had worked out.

As I rode with Crymes to the station house, I considered what had happened.

Obviously, I had missed a tail somewhere on the figure-eight I had driven after dumping Frankie Wu on that dirt road east of Montara. I had a hard time imagining how, because I'm pretty good at catching people on my ass, but there you are. Maybe the tongs had a chopper watching me.

Maybe they used a spy satellite or had the power of invisibility.

Maybe I had just gotten sloppy.

Whatever the case, they had found my car parked a couple of streets over from the Montara house and had seen me leave to drive back to San Francisco, and then they'd entered the house and did god-knows-what to Taylor before cratering his face with the cittern neck.

They'd done all of this while I was in San Francisco eating mussels with Benny Horowitz, congratulating myself for being such a smooth operator.

What a putz.

The mental gymnastics that led me to this conclusion took just about as long as the ride to the Pacifica station. Crymes helped me out of the car, but he waited until we were inside the station to take off the bracelets. I didn't argue with him about it.

"You want a drink or anything?" he asked, after sitting me down in one of interview rooms.

"Got some bottled water?" I said. "I had Italian a couple of hours ago, and I'm a little parched."

"Sure."

He disappeared for a few minutes and returned with a bottle of water and a cola.

"Okay," he said. "I want a detailed account of the last two days. Every minute, from the time Taylor Chu resurfaced and you took him to that place in Montara."

I gave it up. I told him everything, including the search for Cesar Ordonez, the roust by Sung Chow Li, the search for Buddy Wei. I even told him about my meeting with Benny Horowitz. Nobody was served by maintaining confidentiality at this point.

As I told Crymes about the meeting with Benny, I reached into my wallet and pulled out the receipt for the meal at the restaurant. I gave him the name of the place, and told him that the waitress would remember me, because I was eating with the guy who was slipping her the braunschweiger.

He stapled the receipt onto the sheet of paper he was using to take notes.

"When the coroner comes back with the time of death, we'll compare it with the information from the restaurant."

"Well, you'd better add the drive time into the city, and then include the time it took to walk from where I parked—Hong can verify that—to the top of Montgomery Street and back. Then add in the time it took to drive back to Montara, at rush hour. Hong can verify that, too. I left Chu around one-thirty."

"We'll check all that," Crymes said. "What I don't understand, though, is why you hid Chu for two days. The whole fuckin' world thinks he's dead, and you know otherwise?"

"A lot of people knew. Frank Raymond with SFPD knew, the San Francisco coroner, Sung Chow Li, those Hop Sing clowns. Seems like just about everyone had figured it out by the time Chu really did die."

"So, why stash him out here in my precinct?"

"He asked for protection."

"When?"

"Chu showed up at my office a couple of days ago, looking like shit flushed and dredged back up. I let him take a shower and gave him a change of clothes. He was scared to death. He didn't know who had nabbed him, how he'd gotten away, or whether they might try to grab him again. He wanted me to keep him safe. Not many people know about my house here, so I figured it was the perfect place."

One of the uniform cops rapped on the doorsill, and Crymes gestured for him to come in. The cop laid a cloth-wrapped object on the table and leaned over to whisper something into Crymes' ear.

Crymes nodded and patted the cop on the arm.

After the cop left the room, Crymes began unwrapping the object.

"I had the guys in forensics look over your car," he said.

"Tell them to change the oil and rotate the tires when they put it back together."

"Don't be an asshole," Crymes said, pushing the object across the table. "You know what that is?"

It was a small box, about the size of a pack of cigarettes. Three narrow-gauge wires streamed from it. One of the forensic team members had unscrewed the case, exposing a circuit board inside.

"It was in my car?"

"Under it. Attached to the bottom of the backseat well."

"Tracking device of some kind?"

"Better than that. This little baby will not only tell people where your car is, it will let them listen to you as well. There's a very sensitive unidirectional microphone on the surface with the magnet that they use to attach it to the car. It can register your conversations if you're in the car. The homing beacon is tied in to the GPS satellite system. If you were a military target, the Navy could blow a cruise missile right up your ass with this little jewel."

"That's how they found Chu," I said. "They waited for me to park the car, and then they just followed the signal to it, and probably saw me leave the house to go back to San Francisco."

"It sounds reasonable."

"But, if they had the homing dingus, why did they put the tail on me?"

Crymes thought about it for a moment, and then began to wrap the device back up.

"My first impression is that you are one popular fellow," he said. "The hot money says that the Hop Sing didn't plant this on you."

"Sung Chow Li?"

"Possibly. Or, you might want to consider that someone else was also looking for Chu. A third player. Someone you don't know about yet."

There was another knock at the door.

I suppose I shouldn't have been surprised, after everything else that had happened, but I think I must have sat there with my mouth wide open for half a minute.

An Asian gentleman of medium height, wearing a thousand-dollar suit, sporting about ten thousand dollars' worth of dental work, walked into the room, and extended his hand to Crymes.

"Detective, I'm Louis Gai. I'm representing Mr. Gold."

"Whoa," I said. "Excuse me, but..."

"Please, Mr. Gold, you may wish to remain silent at this point."

"What in hell?" Crymes said, glaring at me. "D'you call him from your house while I was investigating...?"

"Mr. Gold didn't call me," Gai said. "I have been retained by Mr. Sung Chow Li to assist Mr. Gold."

He pulled a sheaf of papers from his briefcase and handed them to Crymes.

"You'll find the applicable paperwork for *habeas corpus* in that packet," Gai said. "I'm advising Mr. Gold to make no more statements. If you don't intend to arrest him, this interview is over, and I formally request that you release Mr. Gold. If you do plan to arrest him, the *habeus corpus* paperwork is in order, and I am authorized to pay his bond."

"Judge ain't gonna give bond in a first-degree murder case," Crymes protested.

"Quite so," Gai replied. "However, you still have to convince the District Attorney to charge Mr. Gold with first degree murder, or any other crime, for that matter. You might find that difficult."

He turned to me.

"Do you have transportation back to the city?" he asked me. "Mr. Sung would like to meet with you at your earliest opportunity."

"Wait a minute!" Crymes argued. "You really think you can waltz in here, interrupt an interrogation, and whisk this clown off to San Francisco, just like that?"

Gai's eyes narrowed as he looked down at Crymes. He looked like a cartoon fox.

"Yes, Detective," he said. "That's exactly what I think. I would suggest that you either formally arrest my client at once, or release him. He will answer no more questions."

Crymes was stuck, and he knew it. His evidence against me at this point was completely circumstantial, and I think he'd already done the clock math in his head and knew that I wasn't anywhere near the Montara House when Chu was murdered. He had no choice but to release me.

"Forensic team took my car apart," I said. "I don't know how long it will take to put it back together."

"I can give you a ride to Chinatown," he said. "I'm sure Mr. Sung would arrange for transportation to your home. Detective... Crymes? Will you see to it that Mr. Gold's car is delivered to his home in San Francisco as soon as it is returned to its original repair?"

"What?"

"Mr. Gold, please give your address to Detective Crymes. Detective, I expect that Mr. Gold's car will be at his house by tomorrow morning."

"I could really use some wheels tonight," I said.

"We'll arrange for a loaner," Gai said, and then turned back to Crymes. "Is there anything else that needs to be done here, Detective?"

Crymes started to argue again, but some kind of reason took over. He was way beyond his depth, dealing with a sharpie like Louis Gai, and he was smart enough himself to recognize it.

"Apparently not," he said.

"I want my gun back," I said.

Crymes opened his briefcase and handed the Browning to me across the table.

"When can Mr. Gold take back control of his home in Montara?" Gai asked.

"It'll be a few days," Crymes said. "The place is a crime scene. The forensics team will be working it over thoroughly."

"I have a lot of expensive equipment in there," I said. "There's almost fifty thousand dollars' worth of tools, and the instruments are worth a lot more than that."

"I'm certain that Detective Crymes will provide for safe storage."

Gai handed Crymes a card.

"Detective, please call my secretary when the house is ready to be reoccupied. In the meantime, I suggest that you find suitable storage for Mr. Gold's tools and instruments."

"Air conditioned," I said, noting Crymes' slow burn begin to turn into a brushfire. "The instruments can't handle hot temperatures or high humidity. The glue will fail."

"Temperature-controlled storage, Detective?" Gai said, with a disingenuous smile.

Crymes ignored him and focused on me.

"Gold," he said, "you have burned a bunch of my good will today. I gave you a ton of leeway, and I expect you to inform Mr. Gai here that I did. I'm not about to provide specialized storage for your stuff, but I will assign a uniformed cop to keep an eye on your house until the forensics team is finished, and you can go back in. I will personally guarantee that any tools or instruments not involved directly in the murder will be undisturbed. Will that satisfy you?"

I glanced at Louis Gai, who nodded, maybe half a centimeter.

"Why, yes, Detective," I said. "That will be most satisfactory. May I go now?"

"Could I stop you? Crymes said.

Gai led me out of the Pacifica police station to a Caddy limo parked at the curb. Without saying a word, the chauffeur stepped out from behind the wheel and danced around to the passenger side, where he opened the back door for me.

I slid across the silky leather seats and settled into an agreeable hollow. The other back door opened, and Gai stepped inside, taking the seat facing me. The door closed with more a whoosh than a slam.

"Can I offer you a drink?" Gai asked.

"I'll take some answers," I said.

"I thought as much," he said, as he looked over some papers he had picked up from the seat. "Please allow me to anticipate your questions. I received a telephone call from Mr. Sung about an hour and a half ago. He informed me that you had worked for Taylor Chu, who had been murdered earlier in the day. He asked me to step in for Mr. Chu, whom he presumed would have represented you if he were still alive."

"How did Sung find out that Chu was dead?"

"I have no idea. Mr. Sung did not confide in me."

"Why would he ask you to represent me?"

"Taylor Chu and I had an arrangement. As you are already aware, I took on some of his cases when he disappeared last week."

"Like Chong Lin Kow?"

"That was one of them."

"Chong's dead," I said.

Gai's head jerked away from the papers. I had rattled his cage. I kind of liked the idea that it could be done.

"Say that again."

"Someone killed Chong down near Carmel last night. He was apparently trying to get to Long Beach to get on a container ship bound for Hong Kong."

"How was he killed?"

"Someone shot up his car."

"This is disturbing," Gai said.

"Imagine how he saw it."

"Thank you for the information. I will pass it along to Mr. Sung."

"Why would he care?"

"Beg your pardon?"

"What difference does it make to Mr. Sung if some Chinese tough gets wasted in a road rage drive-by?"

"Mr. Sung asked me to represent Mr. Chong last week. I have no idea what his interest is in the youth. I do suspect he will want to know that he is dead, however."

"You're a cool one, Gai."

"Yes."

"That's it?"

"You are observant and astute. How is that?"

"Damn, you're not just cool, you're cold. Tell me more about this arrangement you had with Chu."

"Why?"

"Because he was my client, and now he's dead, and I figure I ought to do something about that."

"Believe me, there is very little you can do about Taylor Chu's death. The police will be handling it, and I imagine the San Francisco department will want some of it, too."

"Who got tossed off the Bay Bridge last week?"

"I haven't a clue."

I stared out the window as the cookie-cutter houses of Daly City zipped by.

"Makes two of us," I said.

TEN

The limo stopped in Chinatown, at the Yank Sing restaurant on Washington.

"I thought we were going to see Sung," I said.

"Mr. Sung asked me to bring you here," Gai said. "He wanted to meet in a public place."

"What's he afraid of?"

"Many things. At this moment, however, I would imagine he does not want to give the impression that he is engaging in any underhanded activities. I expect that Mr. Sung will be very visible over the next several days."

"You know stuff you aren't telling me."

"Of course I do. Mr. Sung is waiting, Mr. Gold."

"You aren't coming in?"

"I wasn't invited."

He reached into his jacket pocket and pulled out one of those gold-plated business card holders. He slipped a card out of it and handed it over to me.

"Mr. Sung retained me to represent you. I know you have heard of me, and I think I'm the best person to handle your legal affairs now that Taylor has passed on. However, you are free to consult with anyone you wish. If you would need anything, you can reach me at that telephone number."

I stashed the card in my wallet and opened the door.

The limo pulled away from the curb as soon as I shut the door.

I walked into the Yank Sing and was immediately greeted by the same two chowderheads who had invaded my office the day before.

"Mr. Gold," the talkative one named Chan said, and he shook my hand. As he did, he snaked the other hand under my jacket and took my pistol, stowing it quickly and efficiently in his belt. "We'll give it back when you leave. I'm sure you understand."

They escorted me to a table in the far back corner. As soon as I sat a couple of waiters appeared with a folding silk room divider, which they erected around the table.

I sat there for a few moments, and then Sung appeared from behind the panel.

"Sorry to keep you waiting, Mr. Gold," he said. "Business telephone call."

As he sat, the two waiters reappeared, wheeling in two large serving carts filled with plates of dim sum. It seemed that Sung had arranged for his own private all-you-can-eat buffet.

I poured some tea and sampled a couple of the plates. Yank Sing is well known for its dim sum. I had eaten there before.

"I suppose I should thank you for retaining Mr. Gai," I said.

"It was necessary. You have become involved in something unfortunate, and I wanted to assure that you would not be unduly inconvenienced."

"How did you find out that Taylor Chu was dead?"

"Please look under your napkin, Mr. Gold."

I pulled up the napkin and found an envelope. I didn't need to look inside. I could tell by the way it bulged that it was stuffed with cash.

"Are you trying to buy me off?" I asked.

"That's exactly what I'm doing," he said. "You were working for Mr. Chu. Mr. Chu is no longer capable of paying for your services. I have no interest in you pursuing whatever it was Mr. Chu asked you to do. So, yes, I am buying you off. The money should settle all your accounts with Mr. Chu."

I looked at the money, and back at Sung.

"Okay," I said, and slipped the envelope into my jacket pocket.

I didn't give a lot of thought to the morality of it. Some things you leave by the side of the road the minute you hang out a peeper's shingle. A guy comes to you a year after vowing eternal devotion to his soulmate, and asks you to follow her around with no grounds whatsoever for suspicion. The wife isn't doing a thing to warrant being tailed, but you take the guy's money and follow her. You invade her privacy for no other reason than the fact that some guy, missing something elemental in his soul, is incapable of trust. You know your target's innocent, often within ten minutes of taking the job, but you take the money anyway, and you play the voyeur, and you don't give it a second thought.

Sometimes, I find things that bother me. Some guy pays me to follow his wife, he doesn't consider the possibility that I might follow him in the process. If I discover my customer doing something unsavory, like maybe he's keeping a twist on the side and he's planning to divorce his wife, and he wants me to catch her doing something nasty so he can file first, I still take his money.

It's a business thing. I don't do this because I need a hobby. Slogging around in other people's cesspools is the way I pay the bills and buy the exotic woods and specialized tools I use to divert my attention away from the obvious fact that I'm just this big old tattletale for hire.

I stashed the envelope in my jacket, and at that moment the books between Taylor Chu and me were balanced and closed.

That didn't mean I didn't have questions of my own.

"This guy from the Homeland Security, Agent Hong, tells me that Chong Kow is dead."

At first I thought Sung didn't hear me. He reached across the serving trolley and picked up a plate of *shao mai.*

Okay. I could be cool, too. I grabbed a plate of wonton, and ladled a little bit of gyozu sauce over it.

Sung said, "Do you know why the Chinese communists believe they will eventually triumph over the United States?"

"You mean, besides the ever-westward progression of world power?"

"They see it as inevitable. They believe they are superior, and that it is only a matter of time before they achieve control."

"Like Mammy Yokum," I said.

"Excuse me?"

"A character in a comic strip. She used to say '*good is better than evil, because it's nicer.*' The Chinese believe that their natural goodness will overcome the mean, nasty capitalists."

"No, it is more sublime than that. What do you know of Buddhism?"

"Very little. My father was Jewish, and my mother was an Irish Catholic."

"What does that make you?"

"A mutt."

"Do you understand the term *karma?*"

"As a concept? Sure. It's like fate, but more conditional. Things happen because they are bound to happen, as a way of balancing the scales. The world is quartered into active and passive principles, masculine and feminine, and they all have to live together in a one-room apartment. In order to maintain balance and equilibrium, negative acts must be balanced by positive ones. Yada, yada, yada."

Sung stared at me. I think I surprised him.

"Before I was a cop, I was a hippie. I took Eastern philosophy at San Francisco State," I said.

"You surprise me, Mr. Gold."

See? I knew I had.

"Don't let it get to you. I'm a one-trick pony. So, you're postulating the Red Chinese believe that enough bad shit has happened to them that it's about time they got a few bennies out of the deal?"

"That is a concise way of putting it."

"But they don't mind sweetening the pot a little by smuggling large numbers of undocumented immigrants onto our shores."

"No, they don't."

"Or by buying both ends of the Panama Canal, so that nobody enters or leaves without their permission."

"That is one tactic."

"Or by dropping a restaurant on about every corner, so that Jewish families have a place to eat out on Christmas."

"Now you are jesting with me."

"Sorry. What does this have to do with Chong Kow?"

"Much the same as it had to do with Taylor Chu. Both of them became involved in something they didn't understand, which was outside their personal frames of reference. You are part Jewish, you said?"

"My father."

"Have you ever wondered how it was that ten million of your people complied with the orders to be moved out of their homes and cities and placed in camps during the Second World War?"

"That's easy. The other side had more firepower. *My people* were forced."

"They could have resisted."

"They didn't understand what was happening. They thought it was all temporary..." I stopped. "I see what you mean."

"The idea of their extermination was unthinkable to them. It couldn't happen, because it was too monstrous to consider."

"I said I got it."

"I was just reinforcing my point. You know the tongs are associated with Hong Kong triads?"

"Of course."

"And that, in a country almost unilaterally controlled by Communists, the Triads represent unbridled capitalism?"

"That's one way of putting it."

"You can imagine, then, the agenda of the Republic when it took over Hong Kong."

"You were number one on their hit parade?"

"Yes. Fortunately, at least for the moment, all of the former British protectorates have proven resistant to adopting the Communist ways. It is also interesting that, in some sectors, the Chinese communists have begun to embrace, in a very limited fashion, the profit motive."

"So I've heard."

"It is one reason why China was extended Most Favored Nation trading status by the Congress. Now, Mr. Gold, if you are going to engage in capitalist, profit-oriented activities, it should stand to reason that you will want to do business in a place where these activities thrive."

"You're saying that China, with its eighty-gazillion people, is cash-strapped, and wants to do business here in the States."

"No, it wants to *dominate* business in the States. Allowing itself to play by another country's rules is antithetical to China's goals. They believe that they are destined to be in control. It is an expression of worldwide karma, a movement that supersedes the desires, or even the existence, of any single individual. The needs of the many, Mr. Gold."

"Yes. I see. So Taylor Chu and Chong Kow somehow got in the way of this Chinese juggernaut, and got steamrolled."

"A colorful description."

"And you're buying me off because I'm in line to get flattened."

"Let us say that Mr. Chu is no longer an issue, either for me, for you, or in the greater scheme of things. What is happening between Hong Kong and China—and, I might add, the United States—makes their fates, their *karma*, of no more consequence than the fates of those ten million Jews were to the Nazis in Germany."

"There is a flaw in your analogy," I said.

He raised his eyebrows.

"The Nazis got squashed in the end."

"Quite so. They made an error involving the economy of scale. They thought so much of themselves that they forgot they were a small country with a limited population, fighting against a world that was determined to beat them. As you have mentioned already, however, China has eighty gazillion people. There is no inequity in scale weighing against it.

"On the other hand," he continued, "I have a great deal to gain if, as you also said, China gets squashed. The same can be said for all the tongs. I would not like to live in an economic system dominated by an outwardly capitalist, but inwardly Communist, mainland China. In many ways, the tongs act in much the same manner as the Cuban exile community in south Florida. We are a first line of defense against an insidious secret invasion of mainland Chinese being sent here to infect our system."

"I suppose," I said, "that this explains thirty-seven dead, armed Chinese guys in a shipping container in Long Beach."

"I have no idea what you mean."

Like hell he didn't.

"Was Taylor Chu a grass sandal?"

Sung sipped from his water glass, ate a couple of dumplings, and chewed intently. He never looked at me.

After swallowing, he placed his chopsticks on the plate.

"Taylor Chu is no longer a factor. I regret that. I genuinely liked him. He had a lot to offer. I did not have him kidnapped, and I didn't have him killed. The answer to your question is 'no'. Chu was not a grass sandal."

I settled back in my seat.

"He would have been, in a few years, however," Sung said.

"He was being groomed."

"He was being trained. The duties he would have acquired, at some point in the future, would have required the most delicate communications skills. It is important to understand that what you say is no more crucial than how you say it. It is a significant deviation between our two cultures, Mr. Gold. We believe that the value of the individual is enhanced as he ages, and his wisdom is to be exploited. Your culture is shamed and embarrassed by his its aged. In a few years, perhaps, Chu would have made an excellent grass sandal."

"Did he know he was being trained?"

"No."

"Who did know?"

"I have no idea. Many people, perhaps. Most of the Dragon Heads know who is and isn't being watched."

"It's a big deal, being a grass sandal."

"Without going into great detail, they are highly revered."

"They make a lot of money?"

"Why do you ask?"

"One of the rules you learn along the way. Follow the money."

"For instance, the money in your jacket pocket," he said.

"Taylor thought that Chong Kow, or some other individual, had been brought to San Francisco to kill one of the grass sandals."

"So I've heard."

"Was he right?"

"I cannot tell you."

"If one of the grass sandals were to be assassinated, what effect would that have on the tong structure?"

"Are you still investigating this case, Mr. Gold?" Sung asked. "I was direct with you when you asked whether the money I gave you was to buy you out. You are causing me to question my decision."

"This is for my own satisfaction. I'd like to know I was barking up the right tree."

"This is the last question I will answer regarding Taylor Chu," he said. "The murder of an acting grass sandal would have the direst effects on the balance between the tongs in Chinatown. It would trigger a war."

"Well," I said, folding my napkin and dropping it on the table, "this has been fascinating. I'm sorry things ended this way, myself. You can rest assured that matters between Chu and me are settled, and I won't be inquiring further about him. I would like to observe, though, that you seem to have a lot of problems on your hands."

"As always, Mr. Gold. I am sorry that you were drawn into these circumstances. I hope that you will accept my apologies."

"Consider it done," I said, as I stood and pulled on my jacket. "Thank you for the meal, and for the answers you were able to give me. I'll get out of your hair now."

I started to turn but thought better of it.

"Oh, I almost forgot. I have another matter. We discussed it briefly yesterday. I have been asked to locate Buddy Wei by another client. Would following up on that matter mean stepping on your toes?"

Sung wiped his mouth with his napkin and looked up at me.

"Please tell your client that I expect Buddy Wei to turn up in the next couple of days."

I thanked him and offered my hand. He shook it, tentatively. His hand was cool but moist, his grasp almost effeminate. His palms were soft.

His eyes were steely as he took my hand.

I walked back to the front of the restaurant and retrieved my gun from the eloquent chowderhead, Chan, and walked out into the street.

There was a kid in a sportshirt and a pair of khakis standing at the curb, leaning against a new Cadillac Catera. He snapped to attention as I walked out of the restaurant.

"Mr. Gold?" he asked.

"Yes."

"This is your car. It was arranged by a Mr. Gai."

"He had it delivered to the restaurant?"

"He was quite specific. I just need you to sign the delivery sheet."

He held out a clipboard. I signed the sheet, and he ripped of a pink copy.

"Just keep this in the glove box," he said.

"How do I return the car when I'm done with it?"

"Oh, that's no problem. Just call the rental company and tell us where to pick it up. We'll take care of the rest."

He started walking off in the direction of Grant Avenue. I had rented cars before, and I knew he would catch the BART back to the airport.

The keys were in the car. I settled in, started the car, and pulled away from the curb. Compared to my old bucket of bolts, it was like driving the Starship Enterprise.

"Groovy," I said, as I headed toward the Fisherman's Wharf.

ELEVEN

"Bitchin' wheels," *Heidi said* as she stepped out of the gallery.

I had parked the Caddy in front of the building, since it was kind of a shame to hide it in back.

"A little present from Louis Gai," I said. "They're still detailing my car at the Pacifica police station. Want to ride?"

"Sure."

She locked up the gallery and slid into the front seat beside me. I turned the car around and headed back up Hyde toward Russian Hill.

"Radio says Taylor Chu is dead again," she said.

"Yeah, he seems to have a hard time getting it out of his system."

"The radio also said you were being questioned."

"Chu was killed in my Montara house. I don't think it's going to be much of a hassle for me, but I can't go back there for a while. When I do, I imagine I will have to do some major renovations. Fortunately, I can afford them."

I reached into my jacket pocket and handed her the envelope Sung had given me at Yank Sing. She opened it and peered inside.

"Criminy, Gold, do you know how much is in here?"

"Bunches."

She started counting.

"...twenty, twenty-five, thirty, thirty-five... Jesus, there's forty thousand dollars!"

"I can take the rest of the year off."

"What's it for?" she asked, handing the envelope back to me.

"It's for not nosing around Taylor Chu's affairs any more. Sung wants me to leave it alone."

"Are you going to?"

"I took the money. Chu owed me a bunch. It would cost me the rest in time just to try and milk what he owed me from his estate. I figure I broke even."

"But... I mean, damn! He got killed in your house."

"I didn't do it. I wasn't even there."

"Your *sanctum sanctorum*."

I stopped at a light at California and turned to her.

"My *what?*"

"You know what I mean."

"There's a cop named Crymes down in Pacifica who would also appreciate me staying away from the case."

"So, what are you gonna do?"

I fingered the leather-covered steering wheel.

"We could take these bitchin' wheels and drive to Monterey, maybe tour the Hearst Castle at San Simeon, then maybe book it east to Reno or Vegas. Would you like that?"

She snuggled up against me on the bench seat, which was a lot like having a large goose feather mattress roll over you. Heidi is a lot of soft, luscious woman.

"I'd love it," she said. "But I can't. There's nobody to watch the gallery, and I have a new exhibit to put together."

"It'll wait."

"Maybe, but the artist won't. The trip sounds nice, Gold, but I need a little more notice."

"Okay, then, we'll just have to settle for dinner. What about Café Sportt over in North Beach?"

As we drove across Pine to Columbus, I pulled my cell phone from my jacket pocket and punched the speed dial for Wei Ma Lo again. Immediately, the low battery warning beeped and alerted me.

"Oh, hell. Gotta make a detour," I said.

"What's the matter?"

"That Chinese woman who visited me two days ago? She wanted me to find her brother. I've been trying to get hold of her ever since. I guess I'll just have to make it a face-to-face."

I turned south again and drove down Powell to Union Square, where I hung a left on Market and drove into the heart of Chinatown.

"I have spent entirely too damn much time down here," I muttered as I searched for a parking spot near Wei Ma Lo's apartment.

"If you have to park, we could just eat Chinese tonight."

Miraculously, a car pulled away from the curb, just two doors up and across the street from Wei Ma Lo's building.

"Must be my lucky day," I said, as I parallel parked the Caddy, being very careful not to rub the tires up against the curb.

"Luckier than you think," Heidi said, pointing up the street. "There's your client."

I followed her gesture, and saw an Asian woman, maybe twenty-five years old, dressed in a one-piece little black dress, clog heels, with long wavy black hair, walking in a decidedly fluid manner toward the curb. The heels accentuated her long, slim legs, and forced her to thrust out her generous bosom.

"I think you're mistaken," I said. "My client was all business. That's a party girl."

"Men," Heidi said. "You only see what you want to see. That's the girl who was in my gallery. She's just loosened up a bunch."

"Go on."

"Look at her!"

I took another look, and recalled the languorous way she had walked up the steps to my office, and my impression at the time that her staid, business-like appearance had been a shell.

"Damn," I said, and opened the door to the Caddy.

Wei Ma Lo was stepping into a car at the curb, driven by another person. I couldn't see whether the driver was male or female.

"Ms. Wei!" I called.

She didn't turn to look at me. I figured she hadn't heard me over the din of the street.

I started to walk up the sidewalk toward her, but as soon as I got twenty feet away, the car pulled away from the curb.

I raced back to the Caddy.

"What are you doing?" Heidi asked as I chirped the tires pulling into the traffic.

"I can't get her on the phone," I said. "I'm going to follow her."

"Cool! I've never tailed anyone before."

"It's not exactly tailing. I kind of want her to know I'm back here, after all."

I could see Wei Ma Lo's car at the top of the hill as it turned onto Pacific. As soon as I made the same turn, I caught another look at it heading up the hill to the top of the city.

We followed her out Stockton toward the ocean. Her driver turned right at Lincoln and started to cross Presidio near Baker Beach.

"She's heading for the bridge," Heidi observed.

"Seems that way."

"We're following her across?"

"Yep."

"Why?"

"Who knows when I'll run across her again? I've been trying to get her on the phone for two days. She's not very conscientious about returning her calls. Why don't you write down that license number?"

"How come?"

"If we lose her, maybe I can find out who owns that car and get through to her that way."

"You can do that?"

"I have friends at the Civic Center."

I didn't bother to tell her I was planning to take one of them to the 49ers game the next week.

We followed them across the Golden Gate. On the other side, they turned left and drove through Muir Beach, past the entrance to Muir Woods, and up the hill to Mount Tamalpais.

We were in Marin County now, the playground of the seriously rich, those who believed that the hideously inflated real estate prices in San Francisco were simply too ordinary and common to trifle with. This was FantasyLand, the home of Luke Skywalker and Mork from Ork. You couldn't see the houses, but every several hundred feet there were gated drives emptying out onto the PCH, the only external signs of the movie stars, silicon kings, and entertainment moguls who lived on the north side of the Golden Gate.

Wei Ma Lo's car curved around and took a twisting canyon road off the PCH, heading up toward the summit of Mount Tam. I didn't bother lying back, since I wasn't trying to be surreptitious. On the other hand, I was curious as to where she might be heading so decked out and buoyant.

As the residences became less and less dense, I started to entertain a hypothesis.

At last, the car took one last turn, the one I had suspected it might take.

"Well, I'll be damned," I said.

"What?"

"I do not believe this. Snookums, I have a feeling you're in for a real education tonight."

I made the same turn, and climbed the twisting dirt and gravel road that led to a ranging, single level Spanish style home, which was lit up with the approximate candlepower of 3Com Park.

There was a long circular driveway in front of the house, built completely out of glossy, lacquered brick pavers. The car that had brought Wei Ma Lo up the hill was parked near the front door. I grabbed an available parking spot halfway around the circle and shut off the car.

"Hot damn," I said.

"You want to explain what's going on?"

"And spoil the surprise? No way. Come on."

I stepped out of the car and walked around to Heidi's side to help her out. We walked around the circular driveway to the front porch of the house. It was the second overwhelming front door I had seen that day. This one was about sixteen feet high and made from carved Spanish cypress. There was a tendril-like grapevine pattern running between the panels, and the knobs gleamed like pure gold.

I knocked on the door. Several seconds later, a man roughly the size of Oakland opened it. He peered down at us the way Cyclops regarded Odysseus.

"Yeah?"

"I'm here for the show," I said.

"What show, man? I don' know what you're talkin' about."

"Tell Simon Eamon Gold is cooling his heels on the front porch."

Without a word, the giant closed the door, and left me, cooling my heels.

"That's impressive," Heidi said.

"The house?"

"No, the way your name just opens doors. Who's Simon?"

"He owns the house."

The door opened again, and a fellow who more closely approximated my size walked out wearing a huge grin, with his arms opened wide. He was dressed in a flowery Hawaiian surfer's shirt and loosely woven cotton drawstring pants. His head was shaven completely bald.

"Eamon!" he squealed and threw his arms around me. "Who told you we were working tonight?"

"Just a hunch."

He backed off and surveyed my date.

"Heidi Fluhr, Simon Wolf," I introduced.

"My...*Gawd*," he said. "She's *perfect!*"

"See," I said to her, "You wouldn't believe me when *I* told you that."

"I gotta know, sweetie," Simon said, as he reached out and cupped her breasts. "Real?"

I had to hand it to Heidi. She didn't even flinch.

"She's not talent, Simon," I said. "She's my dinner date."

He jerked his hands back as if Heidi's boobs were electrified—which, I realized, was about the only thing they weren't.

"I am *so* sorry," he said to her, and reached out again, this time to give her a hug. She reciprocated.

"You know the most interesting people, Eamon," she said over his shoulder.

"Just wait," I told her.

"Come on in," Simon said, pulling us both by the wrists. "We're shooting tonight, so forgive the mess. There's beer, wine, and booze in the kitchen. We have a nosh table out by the pool. This crowd, you can probably find coke or pot just about anywhere."

"Shooting?" Heidi asked.

"Yes," Simon said. "Look, I have to run finish the setup. You two kids get something to eat and drink. We'll talk later."

He started to run off, but turned just before rounding a corner and mouthed *Perfect* toward me again. I think he was referring to Heidi, but with a guy like Simon, you never know.

"Kitchen's this way," I said, pointing to my right.

We made our way across the living room, which was strewn with heavy cables, toward a kitchen that might have been designed to serve the Democratic National Convention. There was polished steel everywhere we looked, from the Subzero refrigerator to the gleaming countertops. Pots and pans hung from a rack over a steel-topped island, which also contained eight gas burners and a grill.

A plastic tub near the door leading out to the patio was filled with ice and bottles of beer and wine. I grabbed a Michelob out of the tub and motioned toward it.

"Drink?" I asked.

"I'll take that one," she said, pointing toward my Mich. I handed it to her and fished another out of the tub.

"What's going on?" Heidi asked me

A second later a fellow walked in from the patio. He was built like he spent ten hours a week in the gym, which he probably did, and he was stark naked. His improbably huge penis bobbed back and forth as he bent to grab a bottle of chardonnay from the tub.

"'Scuse, me folks. Her Nibs wants some Napa white," he said, and then returned to the patio.

"Oh, Eamon, I am in love," Heidi said, as she watched his clenched buns retreat toward the pool.

"So is he, and I think you both adore the same person."

She slapped my chest. With most women, it's affectionate. When Heidi does it, you wish you had on body armor.

"What's this all about?" she asked. "Is this some kind of swing party?"

"Sometimes," I said. "Simon writes, produces, and directs porno films. He shoots here a lot. Sometimes things get out of hand. C'mon."

I led her out to the patio. The centerpiece there was a kidney-shaped pool, about twenty feet across and thirty feet long. The stamped concrete deck was ringed by a pea-stone garden filled with Western succulents. There were redwood chaises with weather-resistant floral cushions placed strategically around the pool.

Near the diving board, someone had set up a Canon XL-1 professional videotape camera on a sturdy tripod. Halogen lamps were situated all around, hoisted aloft on aluminum poles. Several naked people stood and sat around as Simon spoke with the cameraman. The fellow who had fetched the wine bottle was sitting on a lounge, his legs spread. Between them crouched a topless woman around twenty. She was fellating him mechanically, her eyes closed, her expression bored.

"She's called a *fluffer*," I said. "It's her job to..."

"I can see what her job is."

"Any time you want to step in, I'm sure she'd appreciate a break."

"Don't tempt me."

One of the actresses who had been listening to Simon turned around, and I nudged Heidi.

"Wei Ma Lo," I said, pointing discreetly.

My client was standing about thirty feet away, brushing her hair. She didn't turn directly toward me, but rather stared out into space. She seemed oblivious to the fact that she was totally nude. Her breasts were larger than I had expected, but not pendulous or floppy. Her areolae were cocoa brown, the size of Oreo cookies. Her belly was flat, and her bottom firm and rounded. She had shaved away all her pubic hair. I glanced around and noticed that none of the actors had pubic hair.

Must have been the fashion that year.

"Okay, boys and girls!" Simon yelled. "Let's do this!"

Somewhere, a tech must have thrown a switch. All of the halogen lamps blazed into life at the same instant. Heidi and I both blinked. The temperature on the set rose ten degrees instantly.

"Positions!" Simon yelled.

Wei Ma Lo climbed onto a chaise, straddling the actor whom we had seen being fluffed. Another actor, suitably erect, stood next to the chaise.

"Camera!"

"Speed!"

"And... action," Simon said.

Wei Ma Lo began flailing about, moaning and gasping. The second actor stood next to her and fondled himself. After several seconds, he stepped in and she reached up and pulled him toward her mouth.

"Now, that's coordination," Heidi said, sipping her beer.

"Kinda like rubbing your stomach and patting your head at the same time," I replied.

"So this is your client?"

"Yep."

"How's she paying you?"

"It was cash," I said, "Maybe I should reconsider."

A third actor stepped into the shot, holding his turgid member in his fist.

"We seem to be running low on orifices," I noted, as he eased in behind Wei Ma Lo.

"*Ow,*" Heidi said. "Now, that's gotta sting."

"You couldn't do that?" I asked.

"As recreation? Not a chance."

"She reminds me of that guy on the Ed Sullivan Show, with all the plates balanced on the sticks," I said.

"The *what* show?"

"Ed Sullivan. He was a... oh, never mind."

"How much does she get paid for this?"

"She can afford me. Why, are you thinking of moonlighting?"

"Hmmm..." she said.

"Cut!" Simon yelled. "Let's change the camera setup, okay?"

All three men disengaged, and Wei Ma Lo stood back up. Where she had been moaning hungrily just a moment earlier, now she just seemed tired. She took a hairbrush offered by her makeup tech ran it through her hair again. The male actors looked bored.

Someone handed her a sheer silk robe. She pulled it on, belting it loosely around her athletic frame. She walked over to the table of food and started grazing at the *crudités* tray.

"Gotta talk with my client," I said.

"White man's work is never-ending. I'll try to occupy myself," Heidi said. Her eyes never left Wei Ma Lo's costars.

I sidled up to the table and sampled a couple of the boiled shrimp.

"Imagine my surprise," I said, as Wei Ma Lo turned in my direction.

"Oh, shit." She turned red, all the way from her ears to the exposed cleavage at her chest.

"I figured you'd say something like that. Did you get my messages? I've been trying to reach you all weekend."

"Were you watching?" she said, pointing distantly toward the chaise.

"From a respectable distance, which I should note put me in a distinct minority."

"What you must think of me."

"And how often. Did you get the messages?"

"I've been busy. We've been shooting this feature all over the Bay area."

"One might think your brother would be important enough for you to make time to call."

"I'm not going to apologize, if that's what you want. You work for me."

"For the time being. How long have you been making these movies?"

She looked around. I had seen that look before, usually on the faces of bond skippers I had cornered in an alley somewhere.

"Look, I have to get back to work, okay?"

"Fine. I just thought you might want an update on your brother."

"Eamon!" Simon said, as he walked up. "You've met my new star!"

"Yes, we've been talking about the movie," I said.

"Sugar's going to be bigger than Asia Carrera," he said.

Sugar. Sugar Wei. My mind tripped over all the permutations of her stage name.

"Who's Asia Carrera?"

Simon snaked an arm around Sugar Wei's waist, and pulled her tight.

"The man is *not* a fan," he whispered lasciviously in her ear. "And after getting a look at his date, I can see why. Sure you can't talk her into doing a bit in one of my movies, Eamon? She'd be *really* hot."

"You can ask her," I suggested, "but if I were you I'd put on a flak jacket first."

"You know," he said, poking at his chin with a delicately manicured index finger, "I'm going to do just that."

He pranced off in Heidi's direction. I turned and smiled at my client.

"For what it's worth, and if you're interested, I think your brother is okay."

"What have you learned?"

"I spoke with Sung Chow Li earlier this afternoon."

"Sung Chow Li! Why did you go to him?"

"It was an unrelated matter. I mentioned Buddy, though, and he told me that he expects Buddy to turn up within the week."

"Did he say where Buddy had been?"

"I didn't ask. Some things you don't come right out with. With Mr. Sung, I had a feeling the less I asked the healthier it would be for everyone concerned."

"So, I just wait?"

"Let's say that we have it on reliable authority that he's safe. Beyond that, it's your call. You asked me to find him, and I have a feeling this is about as close to finding him as we are going to get. I don't plan to do any more snooping until we know more. If you want to retain my services, that's fine. It won't cost you much."

"No. That won't be necessary. If Mr. Sung believes Buddy will return shortly, that's good enough for me. Excuse me, I have to get back to work."

She started to walk back toward the chaise, and pulled off the robe as she moved.

"You're welcome," I said, to her back.

TWELVE

"You wouldn't believe what Simon offered me to be in one of his movies." Heidi said as we lounged on the white leather sofa in the living room of Simon Woods' house.

"He's all heart, Simon," I observed. "You should take it. I have it on good authority this art thing is a passing fad."

"Oh, I never could, but Jesus, you can make some cash."

"What if you didn't have to do the sex thing?"

"What, you mean, just stand around with my tits hanging out?"

"Window dressing."

"I don't know. That would be different, I suppose. Would my mother see it?"

"Does your mother collect porn flicks?"

"No."

"Then I'd make a point of sending it to her."

"Oh, Gold, she'd die."

"Could be the perfect murder."

She slapped my chest again. I felt my heart skip a couple of beats. One more pop and I'd need a defibrillator.

We had sat through three takes, mostly the same four-way stuff shot from different angles, and by then it had become a little boring. Sex is one thing when you're doing it, quite another when you're a passive witness. At first, I thought Heidi was a little turned on, but that was probably just her infatuation with the well-hung male lead. After a half hour, I suppose the novelty just wore off.

"Sad," she said, twirling her empty beer bottle and staring down the neck.

"Want another?"

"Sure." She handed me the empty.

I walked into the kitchen, where there was a line for the beer tub. The lights from the pool area had toned down to a dull glow, so I figured they were taking a break.

I grabbed a couple of beers and dropped the caps into the trash. There was another apparent visitor standing next to the can sipping from a glass full of amber liquor on the rocks. I could tell he wasn't talent. For one thing, he wasn't naked, which seemed to be the way most of the actors stayed, and for another he was paunchy, sallow-faced, and in his fifties.

"Beats going to the opera, huh?" he said, as I dropped the caps into the trash.

"Depends on the opera."

He extended his hand.

"Barney Gates."

I almost dropped the bottles.

Coincidences really bother me. Here, out of the blue, I had bumped into the guy Taylor Chu had done a contract for with Sherman Fong. It bothered me.

I placed the bottles on the counter and took his hand.

"I've heard of you," I said.

"Good things?"

"Eamon Gold," I said. "I worked for Taylor Chu."

Maybe it was just chance, us meeting at this shoot. He seemed to blanch a little, and if I hadn't had a firm grip on his palm he might have jerked his hand back as if he'd touched a vial of anthrax.

"Jesus. What a mess. I heard about Taylor on the radio on the way up here tonight."

I decided to have mercy on him. I let him have his hand back. He slugged back a healthy swallow of the highball.

"Then you know where he died."

"Your place, wasn't it?"

He damn well knew it was my place.

"Yeah. It was messy."

"You worked for him?"

"I'm a private investigator. He hired me to do background checks, that kind of thing."

"Sounds exciting."

"Oh, yeah, if you like hanging around the City Clerk's office and the courthouse a lot."

"I guess Chu told you about the matter he was handling for me."

"The way I heard it, he was working for Sherman Fong. You were just the other party."

"A Japanese steak house. You know, one of those places where the cooks grill your food right there at the table."

I nodded. Then I waited for him to tell me more.

There's something terribly intimidating about silence. Most people are used to the give and take of everyday discourse. They expect that when they're done talking, someone else will take up the slack. When it doesn't work out that way, they try to fill the empty spaces themselves. When they do, there's always the chance they'll be more concerned over keeping the conversation lively than they will about what they say.

I kept my eyes on Gates' eyes and waited for him to crack.

He glanced away first, toward the pool.

"How about that Sugar Wei, eh? Is she some kind of hot, or what?"

"You've seen her before? I thought she was new in the business."

"I'm paying her. I've been at all the shoots for this flick."

I waited again.

"I'm the executive producer," he said, finally.

"I don't know what that is."

"Basically, I bankroll the film. The executive producer puts up the money, and the director and the producer put together the film."

"Find the script, hire the actors, that sort of thing."

"I wouldn't know where to start with something like this, Mr. Gold."

"Did you at least get to sit in on the auditions?" I said, grinning like an old conspirator and jabbing at him with my elbow.

"Oh, hell yes!" he said, laughing. "Wooh, was that something."

"I'll bet."

"Have you known Simon Wolf for long?" he asked.

"A few years. He was a client."

"Yeah, what about?"

"About five years ago. Beyond that, I really can't talk about it."

"Oh, yeah, confidentiality and all that."

"I am a Discreet Investigator."

"That's good," he said, nodding. "Yeah, that's good."

"Well, you bet. Especially since, you know, you're sort of a client too."

He looked back at me, just as the halogen lamps went back on around the pool.

"How's that?"

"Well, I worked for Chu, and Chu was handling your contract with Sherman Fong."

"What in hell would Chu need with a private detective on that contract deal?"

I stared at him again, trying to look a little dumb, and maybe a little surprised.

"Oh, man, I'm sorry. I thought Chu kept you in the loop," I said. "Forget it, okay? I'll get back to my date."

I started to turn, but Gates grabbed my arm. He looked flabby and out of shape, but his grasp was firm, and his intention that I wasn't going to leave was clear.

"Chu's dead, Mr. Gold. If you're investigating me for some reason, I want to know what it is."

"Hey, I spoke out of turn, okay? I forgot for a moment that Sherman Fong was Taylor's client, not you. Too much beer, you know?"

"What? You're saying Sherman had me checked out?"

"We're back to that confidentiality thing, Mr. Gates. I really can't talk..."

"The hell you can't."

Mr. Jovial had taken off for the coast. I was seeing Gates' angry side, as his eyes narrowed, and his scowl seemed set in concrete.

"What is it Fong wanted to know?"

"It's not like that," I said, working through the lie, carefully. "Look, you put it together. Fong is planning to joint venture with you on a big project. He's going to put up a hefty chunk of cash, just like you are. Wouldn't you want to know what kind of guy you're partnering with?"

"Fong knows me, damn it."

"Does he know that you're bankrolling fuck films?"

"What the hell does that have to do with anything?"

He was getting loud. People were starting to look our way.

"You might want to keep it down, Mr. Gates," I suggested.

"Like hell. I own this party. You're drinking my beer. I want to know why Sherman Fong was investigating me. We had a deal, even before he went to Taylor Chu. Chu was just supposed to write the contract. Nobody said anything about investigating each other."

"It's all standard procedure. You had an attorney working your end, didn't you?"

He nodded.

"Sure you did. And I'll bet, if you asked him, he tell you he had someone checking out Fong. It's a matter of protecting the client."

Somehow, Simon had materialized at our side.

"Is there a problem, Mr. Gates?" Simon asked.

"You invite this guy?" Gates asked Simon.

"Eamon? He and I are old friends. He doesn't need an invitation."

"Seems he's doing some kind of investigation of me. I don't like him being here."

"Tell you what," Simon said. "Why don't you walk out by the pool, get some air. I'll talk to Eamon. Maybe we can work this all out."

Gates stared me down for a moment, then set his empty glass down on the counter before walking out toward the pool.

"What's this all about?" Simon asked.

"Honest, Simon, I didn't come here looking for him. I didn't even know he was involved with you until five minutes ago."

"Are you investigating him?"

"It's a business thing," I said. I hated lying to Simon, but something was up with Gates, and I had to play the game all the way out. "Nothing to worry about. I thought he already knew about it. I actually came here to see your star."

"Sugar? What's she done?"

"Nothing that I know about. She's a client. I've been trying to reach her all weekend."

Simon put his arm around my shoulders and started to walk me back to the living room.

"Eamon, you know I love you like a brother, and God knows I owe you after what you did for me. This guy Gates, though, he's a hothead, and he's my cash cow right now. I really would like to keep him happy."

"Don't worry about it," I said. "I already told Sugar what I came to say. We don't have to stick around."

"It's not like that," he said, squeezing my shoulder. "You and Heidi stay as long as you want. I'll handle Gates. Just try to stay out of his way."

"I never tried to get in his way. I did promise to take Heidi to a nice dinner tonight, though. Maybe we ought to get back to the city before they roll up the sidewalks."

"You come back whenever you want. You got that? And make sure you bring Heidi. I'm not finished recruiting her."

I said goodbye, and Simon hustled back to the patio to set up the next shot.

"Where's my beer?" Heidi asked.

"We'll get you another one at the restaurant. Think you've seen enough?"

"Enough to give me ideas for after dinner. What's the rush?"

"Something's up with this guy Gates. I'd like to give it a look-see."

"Whatever," she said, raising herself from the couch. "Long as you buy me dinner first."

I walked her out the front door and helped her into the Caddy. I was circling around the front of the car, toward the driver's side, when I saw Barney Gates jogging in my direction. I stood by the car until he got there.

"Look, Gold, I'm sorry for losing it in there," he said, his voice choking a little from the exertion of running to catch me. "I didn't mean to muscle you around."

Like he could.

"Don't worry about it," I said.

"That's not the only reason I came out here. Simon told me you came here to see Sugar Wei. Maybe meeting me was just this crazy accident, you know?"

"Yeah, maybe."

"It's just that, you see, I really don't want to queer this deal with Sherman Fong. It's one thing to have a couple of restaurants between here and wine country. It's totally another thing to have one in downtown San Francisco. This movie thing, it's just a big tax dodge. I need a couple of losing efforts to bring down my bill to Uncle Sam. That's all it is. I'd hate for Fong to get the wrong idea."

"Like, maybe, you're a sex-crazed perv who likes to take sloppy sixteenths with college-aged porn stars?"

"Well, I wouldn't put it that way, but I can see how Fong might take it like that."

"What are you saying, Gates?"

"You didn't come out here to see me tonight, that's fine. Let's leave it there."

"I didn't meet you here?"

"Something like that."

"I should just forget I ran into you."

"Hell, man, who are you gonna report to anyway? Chu's dead. He was a one-man operation. I'd imagine Sherman's gotten himself a new lawyer already. You know, someone who has his own investigator."

"I should just drop it."

"I'd make it worth your while."

I stared at him.

"Oh, come on, Gold. I'm sure you've pulled down some expenses on this thing. You want to think about how long it's gonna take to suck that out of Chu's estate."

I thought about the money weighing down the left breast pocket of my jacket. I had used the same reasoning earlier in the evening, myself.

On the other hand, it represented actual work I had done trying to find out who kidnapped Taylor Chu. I hadn't really done any work on the Fong-Gates contract.

"Forget it," I said, clapping him on the shoulder. "Let's call this a freebie."

"No word to Fong?"

"He won't hear it from me. Okay?"

We shook on it, and he started to amble back to the house. I climbed behind the wheel of the Caddy and started the engine.

"Dinner?" I asked.

"Sure," Heidi replied. "Maybe afterward, we can find a nice opium den somewhere."

THIRTEEN

After dinner, I dropped Heidi off at her place, with a vague suggestion that I might be back later in the evening.

As soon as she cleared her front door, I pulled out the cell phone and called Frank Raymond.

"You sure you got the right guy?" he said. "Sure you don't want Crymes down in Pacifica?"

"You have a right to be sore," I said. "But I was just following my client's wishes. You know how the confidentiality thing works."

"Well, we'll never know now, will we? What do you want, Gold?"

"Can you get me into Taylor Chu's office?"

"What for?"

"It doesn't have anything to do with his murder, if that's what you mean. You confiscated all my files the other day. I didn't copy everything, just the stuff I thought might be relevant to him being snatched. Some things have come up since then, other case stuff that I'd like to check out."

"Don't tell me you're still working his cases," Raymond said. "'Cause I have a feeling he's not going to be paying you anything."

"I work for a lot of people, Frank. Some of them are still breathing. Sometimes their cases and Taylor's overlapped."

"And you don't plan to tell me who these living clients of yours are?"

"Confidentiality. It's a bitch, man."

"Give me something, then. Sweeten the pot a little."

"I already gave the whole thing to Crymes."

"Yeah, and Chu was killed down in Montara, which is his district, but he was kidnapped in the City, which is mine. You're not the only one with overlapping cases, Gold. Tell me something, and maybe it'd be worth my time to get you into Chu's files."

"How about I give you everything I gave Crymes today?"

Twenty minutes later, I was outside Frank's house on Ashbury. He locked the front door and slid into the Caddy with me.

"New wheels," he observed.

"It's a rental. They're still working over my car in Pacifica."

"Pacifica department didn't spring for this."

"No, this is from Sung Chow Li."

"You Sung's fuck buddy now?"

"Nothing of the sort. I didn't even know it was being arranged. Louis Gai set it up."

"Man, I like this less and less. How are you mixed up with Gai?"

"Would you believe he's my attorney?"

"Somehow, I think I'm getting this story ass-first. Maybe you should start at the beginning."

I pulled away from the curb and told him the whole thing, just the way I had with Crymes earlier in the day. Crymes is a decent cop, but Frank is smarter. He makes connections faster. Sooner or later, Crymes would catch up with him, but Frank saw patterns right away that Crymes had missed.

"Let me get this straight," he said. "You got thirty-seven dead Chinese nationals in a shipping container in Long Beach, this Chong character dead in a car south of Monterey, Taylor Chu dead in your Montara house, and five-eighths of some unidentified Asian on a slab down at the morgue."

"That's the story so far."

"Way I see it, the guy got tossed off the Bay Bridge is either Buddy Wei or this Chuck Loo fella."

"Technically, it's Chuck Fat."

"Whatever."

"How do you figure it's one or the other?"

"Chuck Loo/Fat drops by Sung Trucking on Monday to sign checks and hasn't been seen since. Buddy Wei goes out to a movie on Monday night and disappears. Taylor Chu gets nabbed on Monday. Busy day."

"Sung says Chucky is in LA doing a moving job," I said.

"So, he turns up in a day or so, we know the floater was Buddy Wei."

"What about the other two, Sammy Chin and Lanny Gow? The guys the girl at Sung Moving said were on another moving job?"

"Think they may have headed south too?"

"What's your point?"

"Sung claims that Chuck Fat/Loo is in LA. LA's not far from Long Beach."

"No, man, that doesn't make sense."

"Why not?"

"You're thinking maybe Chucky met up with Chin and Gow in LA and they went to Long Beach to pull off the massacre at the Xinhua Voyager."

"Something like that. Hell, for all we know, Buddy Wei is in it with them."

"Buddy quit Sung Moving a couple of weeks ago. He never collected his last check."

"Okay, so Wei isn't in on the Long Beach job. Doesn't mean the other three didn't do it."

"What about Chong Kow?"

"Damn, you wanna give me some kind of score card here, Gold? I can't keep up with all these slant names."

"Chong Kow is the kid Taylor Chu was appointed to represent on the charges of assaulting Chucky Loo."

"Chucky Fat."

"Whatever. Louis Gai told me that Sung hired him to represent Chong when Taylor disappeared. Taylor told me that Chong was here to do some real damage to the tongs by killing one of the grass sandals. If Chong was working for Sung, and so were Chucky, Lanny, and Sammy, then who killed Chong?"

"Who cares?"

"Don't you see? Chong was headed for the Xinhua Voyager when he was killed. So he was either trying to get out of the country, like James Hong figured, or he was part of the plan to kill the thirty-seven stowaways. If we know who killed Chong, we have a line on..." I stopped.

"What's wrong?"

"Damn. Now I'm lost. This is all screwy, Frank. It doesn't make any sense."

"Since when did anything make sense down in Chinatown? Place is weirder than SoMa. Just pull into the parking garage over here. We'll take the elevator from the lobby."

Taylor Chu's office was on the twentieth floor of one of the office buildings bracketing the Courthouse. It was like a hive of law offices. Attorneys don't like to get too far from where the judges hang out. I drove into the parking garage and headed for the block of spaces reserved for Taylor Chu. I parked in his personal space.

"Man, doesn't that give you chills or anything?" Frank asked.

"He isn't going to use it."

"Parking in a dead guy's space before he's even good and stiff. Jesus."

We walked through the revolving doors leading from the parking garage to the lobby and took the elevator to the twentieth floor. The doorway to Chu's office was barred with yellow crime scene tape. Frank yanked it away and pulled a ring of keys from his pocket. I had seen the ring before. He kept all the keys relevant to active cases together, the same way a real estate agent did for listed homes.

Taylor Chu's office was immaculate, just the way he had left it the night he was kidnapped. The furniture was leather and fine wood, and his desk, an oblong walnut affair, was crisp and tidy. There was just the slightest tinge of dust on top of it, settled since the office had been sealed the previous week.

"We left the file cabinets unlocked," Frank said. "Just in case we had to come back."

He pulled the chair out from behind Chu's desk and sat in it.

"Now who ought to be getting chills?" I asked, and pulled the top cabinet out.

"So, what are you looking for anyway?"

"Just some contract stuff. Taylor was handling some mergers that involved some other clients, and I was working both sides of the fence, doing background checks."

It was a pretty decent lie, all things considered.

"What'd you make last year, Gold?"

"Why? Thinking of going private?"

"I got a gold shield, eighteen years on the job, and the house is almost paid for. You think I'm gonna jump ship now? Two more years and I can punch out with a full pension. Talk to me then. Really, though, what'd you score last year?"

I found Taylor's file on Sherman Fong. Actually, there were three files. Taylor had done a lot of work for Fong, which didn't surprise me. I recalled that he had told me he and Fong had grown up together, had known each other for thirty years.

I also recalled that Kevin Krantz had referred to Fong as being *all tonged up*.

Curiouser and curiouser.

I took the Fong files and sat in one of the chairs across from Frank.

"Let's just say that the free enterprise system has been kind to me," I said, as I began looking over the chart. "Like you, my houses are paid for, and I don't have any dependents. I do all right. The difference is, I don't get to quit after twenty years. No pension."

"What, you got no IRA? No Keough?"

"Slipped my mind."

The first of the three files appeared to cover work done for Sherman Fong between 1980 and 1990. It was mostly contract work. There was a copy of Fong's will, some medical power of attorney documents he had done before going in for surgery in 1984, and several real estate deals.

One contract, a joint venture in 1988, grabbed my attention. It was a strip mall deal Fong had worked with a guy from Fresno.

The guy from Fresno was represented by Louis Gai.

I started flipping through the file, checking out each contract. Between 1988 and 1990, Taylor Chu had handled ten contracts for Sherman Fong. Five were partnership deals involving merging capital to do something big - a restaurant here, a shopping center there, a couple of apartment buildings. In each case, the partner was represented by Louis Gai.

I picked up the second file, running from 1991 to 1999. It took a few minutes, but I counted fourteen joint venture contracts, in which Sherman Fong was represented by Taylor Chu, and the other partner's attorney was Louis Gai.

The third file, thinner by far, covered all the years since 1999, and included a copy of the contract Taylor had been working on between Fong and Barney Gates. I already knew what I would find, but was still a little rattled when I discovered that Gates was represented by Gai.

"Damn," I said.

"Find something?"

"I don't know. What's your impression of Louis Gai?"

"He's the guy they invented lawyer jokes for."

"Come again?"

"Y'know, like, '*What do you have when you put twenty lawyers at the bottom of the ocean - a good start*'. That kind of joke."

"You don't like him."

"Hell, nobody does. You don't. No cop that's been grilled by him on the stand likes that son of a bitch."

"That's just it, isn't it? We all know Louis Gai from the courtroom. The guy is a defense attorney, a litigator, does almost all criminal stuff."

"Yeah?"

"Now, I can understand if Taylor was doing some favors for Sherman Fong, doing some contracts here and there. They had been friends since before disco. But what is Gai doing all this contract work for? And for so many different people?"

"I don't follow."

"I've looked at something like twenty different business partnership contracts stretching over the last twenty years or so, all involving Sherman Fong and different business partners. Not four or five different partners. All of them different partners. Each and every one of the partners was represented by Louis Gai."

"Sweetheart deal," Frank said.

"What?"

"What you got here is your basic butt buddy arrangement. If you ask me, Gai and Chu were in it together. Chu has Sherman Fong all tied up. Who else is Fong gonna run to if he needs some contract work done? All the lawyers in this town know each other. Fong goes to some other guy, Chu's gonna hear about it. So, Gai scouts around, finds some pigeon looking to move into the bigtime south of the Golden Gate, and he brings the mark to Chu. Chu tells Fong he's heard of this business opportunity, and Fong ought to jump all over it while it's hot. Chu handles Fong's end, Gai handles the pigeon's end, everybody makes money, nobody's unhappy."

"Nothing illegal there," I said. "Business brokers do it all the time."

"Didn't say it was illegal. It's kind of unethical, if Fong and the pigeon aren't in on the game."

"You know, I think Gai may have said something about this. He told me this afternoon that he and Chu had some sort of arrangement."

"Well, there you are."

"So, we have Sherman Fong, who is all tonged up. We have Louis Gai, who Sung runs to the minute he hears that

Chu is dead. Sung was all in a hurry to assure Chu that the
Sung Chow Li tong wasn't in on the kidnapping, and
apparently knew almost before you did that Chu wasn't
dead."

"Lotta tong shit going on all around Chu for him not to
get a little on him."

"But maybe he didn't know about it."

"How do you figure?"

"I asked Sung directly this afternoon whether Taylor Chu
was a grass sandal. Sung said he wasn't but he was being
groomed for it. I asked Sung if Taylor was aware of it, and he
told me that Taylor didn't know."

"So, who knew?"

"The Dragon Heads."

"What about the other grass sandals?"

"It would make sense."

Raymond scratched his head and stared at the ceiling.

"So, Louis Gai has Taylor Chu all bound up in tong shit,
only he doesn't let him know it's all part of the plan."

"You think Louis Gai is a grass sandal?"

"I know someone who can find out."

"You might want to do that. Look, Frank, I didn't come
here to work on the murder case. I really only wanted to
check out this guy Sherman Fong is partnering with. I... I
can't touch Taylor's case anymore. You understand?"

"Someone's threatening you?"

"No. It's not like that."

"Well, you're not following up on some guy who got
killed in your own house, you're either being threatened or
bought off."

I didn't say anything. I just got up and put the files back
into the cabinet.

"Oh," Frank said.

FOURTEEN

I woke the next morning to the realization I was suddenly unemployed. With Taylor Chu dead, and Sugar Wei telling me she didn't want me to look for her brother Buddy any more, I was fresh out of clients. Maybe Doogie Portnoy would call later in the day with a skip trace for me to handle.

Maybe I'd be out of the office.

I had forty thousand dollars to play with, which said I didn't have to answer the phone for a while if I didn't want to. On the other hand, being a private cop tends to be a sort of momentum-driven business. If you let it slide too long, you're back at the point of building your client base.

Forty thousand. I hadn't seen that much cash in one place in years. Dropping it into my bank account was a bad idea. Any deposit over ten thousand raises a red flag at the IRS. Dump forty large into your average checking account, and you're begging for an audit the next spring.

I rang up Benny Horowitz for some investment advice, but all I got was his voice mail. I hoped he was out scoring my football tickets. The light on my answering machine was flashing, so I hit the replay button.

"Gold, this is Crymes. Just wanted to let you know that the crime scene guys are finished with your house. The car's gonna take some more time to put back together. We got a couple more things come in overnight. Hope this isn't gonna put you out much."

I dialed the number for the Pacifica PD. I was lucky. Crymes was in.

"That was quick," I said.

"I didn't want to tie up a perfectly good beat cop looking after your shack," he said.

"Find anything interesting?"

"This is an active case and last time I checked you're a private citizen."

"Meaning you aren't going to tell me anything."

"You'll be informed if we need more information from you."

"Just a thought, Crymes. Do you want the walls and carpet from the bedroom?"

"Whatever for?"

"You know these beach places. The walls are just paneling nailed to the wall studs. I figure it'll be less labor-intensive to pull down the paneling and roll up the carpet rather than try to clean everything up. I can replace it all in an afternoon. Just thought you might want the stuff I pull down, like you might want to reconstruct the scene later on."

"Now, there's a great idea. I can send a coupla guys over to your place to pick up your trash, so we can haul it down to our brand new thirty-thousand square foot evidence laboratory where we reconstruct entire rooms from crime scenes, just like they do on *CSI*. Who the hell do you think we are, the NTSB?"

"A little early in the morning for sarcasm, Crymes. I was just trying to be helpful. May I presume my alibi checked out?"

"Yeah, you're in the clear. Waitress at that guinea joint in North Beach vouched for you, and being in the custody of the INS at the time the body was discovered was a neat trick. We know you didn't do it. So go ahead and junk whatever you pull out of your house. We've gotten all we need from it."

"You might be getting a call from Frank Raymond. He's working the Chu case from the kidnapping angle in the City."

"Always happy to oblige my brother cops."

Which, I realized, didn't include me.

I decided it was a good time to leave him to his job.

After hanging up, I called a friend of mine who works for a home supplies business and ordered fifteen four by-eight lauan wall panels, and a new roll of tan carpet for the bedroom floor. It occurred to me the bed was pretty much shot, too, so I called the furniture store in Pacifica and asked them to deliver a new frame, mattress, and box springs. I could stop by WalMart and pick up pillows and sheets later.

I called Benny Horowitz and got his voice mail again.

"Hey, Benny, just checking on those 49ers tickets. Also, I just came into some hefty cash I have to plow into some solid investments. Give me a call at the Montara house when you get in."

I left the number for the beach place, and then dressed for physical work, in a pair of patch-legged jeans and a cutoff Giants sweatshirt.

It was a genuinely gorgeous day in the Bay area, so I rolled down the windows in the Caddy and popped a Stones CD into the player while I bopped down the PCH toward Montara.

My guy from the home store was waiting for me when I arrived. I helped him unload the paneling and the carpet. He took an imprint from my credit card and reminded me to call anytime some guy got whacked in my bedroom.

The house was a mess. The Pacifica forensic guys had glopped about a gallon of fingerprint dust in the kitchen and the bedroom, but my shop was the worst. There was dust on the tool chest, the workbench, and on some of the tonewood I had stacked next to the bench. A lot of my tools were coated. As I had expected, my rosewood-handled knives were gone.

I picked up a copy of the Rockler catalog and called to order some new knives, secure in the knowledge that I'd never see my old ones again. If I hadn't been faced with so much work renovating my beach house, I'd have taken the Caddy for a drive over to Luthiers' Mercantile in Healdsburg to pick them up personally, but that would have to wait.

I pulled a pry bar from underneath the workbench and went to work in the bedroom. The sheets had been pulled from the bed after Taylor Chu was taken away, and lay in a pile on the floor.

There was blood everywhere. I had almost forgotten, in less than a day, how Taylor had been butchered. Spatters had hit just about every wall - not a tough feat, considering the room was about twelve feet square, but it was still a mess.

I started to pull the bed apart and then thought better of it. The blood on the sheets, mattresses, and walls was pretty much dried, but I recalled that Hepatitis B virus could live for up to a week. I got one of my dust masks from the workshop and a pair of rubber gloves from the kitchen before starting in to work.

It took a half hour to haul the sheets, pillows, mattress, box springs, and bed frame out to the curb to be picked up. The wall paneling came down in another hour, and another to pull out the various nails left behind. Finally, I yanked the carpet up and rolled it to drag out to the corner. What was left looked a lot like an unfinished walk-in closet, or the petrified remains of some prehistoric Rubik's cube.

I had just finished nailing up one wall's worth of the new paneling when the doorbell rang. It was the guy from the furniture store. I didn't want to drag my new bedding through the workshop just yet, only to get it covered with fingerprint dust, so we decided to just unload the stuff and leave it in the carport.

It took another two hours to finish nailing up the paneling.

I stopped to drink a beer, before starting in on cleaning up all the dust. Fingerprint dust is some kind of fine carbon powder, really nasty stuff that congeals into a paste if you get it wet. An inexperienced guy might have attacked it with a rag and a bottle of 409, and that would have been a real disaster. I started out with my shop vacuum, and the little nozzle wand, and sucked up as much of the muck as I could manage. The rest I went after with a dry rag, until I had about ninety percent of it cleaned up. That was about as good as I could expect. The rest was already caked into corners and crevices around the workbench, and there was no hope of coaxing it out. It would eventually be absorbed and cleaned along with other household dirt.

Cleaning my tools took the longest. Crymes' crew had figured, probably correctly, that if the killer had used my knives to torture Chu, they had probably touched a lot of other stuff while looking for them.

After the workshop was relatively dust-free, I dragged in the carpet and rolled it out on the bedroom floor, using a small fretting hammer to attach it to the tack strips, which I had decided to reuse.

It was only mid-afternoon, and I had succeeded in removing virtually all traces of Taylor Chu's messy departure from my home. Now all that was left was the nagging memories.

I set the new bed up, but decided not to put on sheets just yet, since I didn't plan on sleeping over.

Instead, I went back to the shop and started working on a new cittern neck. There was an ample supply of relatively quarter-sawn hard maple boards in one corner, from which I selected a piece that looked as if it had some nice flame. I pulled down the cittern neck pattern from its nail on the wall, and drew out three quick outlines, which took about half an hour to cut on the bandsaw. On my assembly table, I aligned the laminates and glued them together, then clamped them to dry.

It was time for another beer.

As I sat on the couch and drank, I considered what I might do with some spare time. I could live for quite a while on forty thousand dollars, but it would make more sense to enhance my cash flow with bits and pieces parceled out in monthly dividend statements after Benny Horowitz plowed it into some nice triple-A rated muni bonds. It wouldn't be a lot of money, but it would be free, and at the end I'd still have my forty large. I figured the annual return would run about three thousand, which wasn't bad. Despite what I had told Frank Raymond, I don't make a fortune bird-dogging cheating spouses and doing background checks and tracing skips. A few thousand would make a nice little bit of icing on my fiscal cake.

The telephone rang. I figured it was Benny returning my call.

"Gold," Frank Raymond said, when I picked up the receiver.

He didn't sound happy.

"Yeah."

"I need you to hop into town, come on over to your office."

"What's up?"

"Just get over here, okay?"

I hung up the phone, locked up the house, and hustled north on the PCH into the city. It was right at the beginning of rush hour, which means that everyone who worked downtown was headed out toward San Bruno, or Pacifica, or Daly City. Most folks can't afford to live in San Francisco proper. Anyway, I was driving mostly against traffic, and I hit the top of Hyde Street at California about a half hour after leaving the beach.

The crest of Hyde is one of the most scenic places in the City. You reach the top of the hill, and there's this long ski jump down into the Bay, with the Golden Gate Bridge on the left, Sausalito on the right, and Alcatraz straight ahead. You can look right down at the Hyde Street Pier, and if the fog hasn't rolled in yet it's like a million-dollar picture postcard.

I can also see my office from the top of the hill, it being situated about half a block from the pier. As I topped the hill, I could see it surrounded by lots of blue and red flashing lights. My stomach dropped to the floorboards, and it wasn't because of the incline.

My first thought was of Heidi.

FIFTEEN

I parked in front of the building, beside a bubbletop. I didn't worry about getting a ticket. The cops had the whole block of Hyde Street cordoned off.

I got out of the Caddy and tried to see through the front glass of Heidi's shop as I ran across the street to the office. There were a lot of people in the shop. None of them looked like serious art collectors.

Frank and Dexter Spears met me at the door.

"Is it Heidi?" I asked.

"Relax, Gold. She's okay."

"I want to talk with her."

"She's okay, all right? We're interviewing her now. You can talk with her in a few minutes."

"What's going on?"

"This is business now. Understand? I'm a cop and I have to treat you like you don't know shit. I need you to tell me everything you've done since you dropped me off at my house last night."

"What in hell?"

"Just do it, Eamon."

Raymond didn't often call me by my given name. We had been partners for years, cruising the dingy, hard-assed streets of SoMa, but he still preferred to call me by the family name. When he used Eamon, I knew he meant business.

"I went to Heidi's place. I was there until about two or three. Then I went home."

"Montara?"

"Russian Hill. I got up about eight. I called Crymes from the house, and I called the building supplies place and a furniture store. Then I drove down to Montara to refit the beach house."

"Anyone see you there?" Spears asked.

"Yeah, the two delivery guys. I redid the entire bedroom and cleaned up all the mess from the Pacifica forensic team. You and I both know how long that would probably take, so I had to be there the whole time. What in hell's happened, Frank? Is Heidi really okay?"

"She's fine. Just shaken up. It was a hell of a shock."

"What was?"

"Come with us."

He and Spears led me by the cops standing guard at the door leading to the steps to my office, and we walked up. There was another cop at my office door, which was wide open.

There were two bodies lying on the floor of my office. Three more people, all breathing, stood around making notes and taking photographs.

"Jesus," I whispered.

"Your girlfriend got into work this morning, saw your door open, and decided to pay you a visit." Spears said. "She didn't stay long. Called the PD, screaming that someone had killed her guy in his office. She figured one of these two stiffs was you."

I was too busy trying to be objective, to figure out how two dead guys had managed to find their way onto my carpet, to be irritated at Spears. Somehow, though, the gears in my head wouldn't mesh.

I walked around the first body, taking care not to step in any splotches of blood on the carpet, then knelt in front of him.

"Oh, man," I said. "Oh, Jesus, Frank. This is Benny Horowitz."

"You know him?"

"He was the guy I had lunch with in North Beach yesterday. Ten bucks says you'll find a couple of tickets to the 49ers game Sunday on him."

One of the forensics geeks looked up.

"How'd you know that?" he asked.

"You found them?"

"In his jacket pocket."

"Benny had a way of finding things. I asked him to get me a couple of tickets yesterday. I promised to take a friend to the game. He told me he'd drop them by the office. Jesus, Benny."

Frank put his hand on my shoulder.

"What about the other guy, Eamon?"

I shuffled around and took a long look at him.

"I can't be absolutely sure," I said. "But he looks a lot like the picture I had of Buddy Wei."

Frank nodded.

"I had a feeling he'd show up sooner or later."

"What's your take on this, Frank?"

"I'm still getting a feel for it. I don't like it that you were all by yourself for about six hours last night."

"Get real. You and I did a lot of crime scenes over the years. This happened almost twenty-four hours ago."

"Really."

"Yeah, really. The lividity of the bodies, the way the blood's all dried on the carpet, the smell. This happened either while I was with Heidi at Simon Wolf's house in

Mount Tam, or while I was with you last night. Also, Buddy Wei was killed somewhere else and brought here."

"You a medical examiner now?" Spears asked.

"Don't have to be. Wei's lying on his back, but look at the way his face is all black and blue. That's not bruising. It's blood settling. He was belly down for a long time after he died."

Frank looked over at the forensic geek, who nodded agreement.

My head was beginning to clear, and all the machinery was meshing the way a good cop's thinkworks are supposed to do.

"Someone killed Wei elsewhere, and came up here with him to wait for me. Whoever did the killing didn't know me. They left the door to the office open. Benny came here, like he told me he was going to, to deliver the tickets. He saw the open door, figured I was inside, and came on up the stairs. He walked in, the killers zipped him, and left him on the floor next to Wei."

"Why?" Frank asked.

"Because it's screwy, Frank, that's why."

"Come again?"

"Like we were saying last night. Everything about this case is screwy. Nothing makes sense. Everything's conflicted. If I'm found dead in the same room with Buddy Wei, it just muddies everything ven further."

"So they really intended to kill you, not this Horowitz guy?"

"Benny hadn't been in my office five times in the past six years. There was no reason to expect him to show up."

I pointed to my dead buddy on the floor.

"That was supposed to be me."

Frank and Spears asked me some more questions, mostly confirming stuff I had already told him, and they took down the names of the guys I had spoken with that day. I could tell that Frank really wanted me to be clean in this thing, but at the same time he was becoming a little irritated at the way bodies were piling up around me. Spears just wanted to nail me. I knew he couldn't do it, so I ignored him.

After they finished with the questions, they let me see Heidi. She was in her shop downstairs, sitting in a chair in one corner, sipping from a glass of ice water. Her eyes were red and her makeup was streaked, and she looked like a Norwegian Venus in spite of it all.

As soon as she saw me she jumped up and hugged me.

"Oh, Jesus, God, Eamon, I thought it was you," she sobbed.

"It's okay," I said. "I'm all right."

"What's happening? Why is all this stuff happening?"

"I don't know. Maybe someone thinks I'm onto a trail, and they want me off of it."

"D'you still want to take that vacation?" she asked. It was almost like a plea. "We could just take off, go somewhere far away. I don't give a damn about the gallery right now. I can close up for a week or two. We could just go away, somewhere nice and quiet and hundreds of miles from Chinatown."

"Sounds nice," I said. "But I can't. Not now. Maybe yesterday, or last night, but not now. Not with Benny dead."

"I don't understand."

"It was supposed to be me. Whoever did the double-tap up in my office last night thought they were zagging me, not Benny. Here I was, off playing Sam Spade in Mount Tam with you and Barney Gates, and Benny was paying the freight for my laziness. I can't take off now. Someone has to answer for Benny, you see?"

"What is this?" she said, pulling away from me. "Some kind of man thing?"

"If you like it that way, okay."

"That's just stupid. You don't have a clue who's trying to kill you, and you're ready to just run around kicking sand in everyone's face until someone takes you on."

"Sometimes that's the only way to do it," I said. "Are you all right? I mean, really all right?"

"I took a couple of valiums about a half hour ago. In a few minutes, I'll be fine."

"Then let me take you home. You can get some sleep while I check out a few things. Will you do that?"

She seemed to soften a little. Maybe it was my deadly charm.

Maybe it was the benzos.

"Will you come by later?" she asked.

"I'll try to," I said. "Let's just lock up and get you home. The cops will be here for the next several hours. All we can do is get in their way."

Heidi was nodding off before we got to her house. I tried to figure out just how many milligrams it would take to knock out a big healthy girl like her, and finally settled on *a lot.*

I walked her up to her apartment, helped her undress, and snuggled her under the bed covers. For a long moment of indecision, I considered staying there with her, but my damnable sense of duty wouldn't let me.

"You're coming back?" she said, as I stood to leave. Her voice was getting slurred and hoarse, like Betty Bacall after half a fifth of scotch.

"I'll try to," I said again. "I just have some things to do."

I let myself out, after setting her alarms, and drove the Caddy over to Chinatown. I had the card with Sugar Wei's address on it, and I hoped she wasn't off in the hinterlands getting quiffed by some stud for the cameras.

I parked in a pay lot a block down from her place. She lived two flights up, in an apartment over a discount camera and luggage store. The aroma of chicken broth, frying cabbage, and ginger wafted down the stairs as I walked in the street level door. The stairway was narrow and steep, and the hallway at the top of the stairs was dank and dingy. Sugar was in apartment 3-F.

I knocked on the door. At first, it sounded as if nobody was at home. Then, I heard something drop on the floor, and the shallow thud of bare footsteps.

"Who is it?" someone said from the other side.

"Eamon Gold," I said.

There was a clanking sound of the deadbolt lock being thrown, and the door swung open.

Without her movie makeup and her poofed out hair, Sugar looked small and bucolic, like something out of a Pearl Buck novel.

"I have to come in, Sugar," I said.

She didn't answer. She just let the door fall open farther and walked away from me. She was wearing loose silk pajamas, and nothing else, a fact I detected readily as she walked in front of the window.

"I have some bad news," I said, as I closed the door.

"I know," she said, as she collapsed on a chaise near the television. "The block tong representative came by about an hour ago."

Now I knew why she wasn't made up. Crying would have destroyed any cosmetics she might have been wearing.

She sounded stuffy and nasal. She sniffed as she turned to look out the window.

"I need some answers," I said.

"Like I have any?"

"You're a good place to start. I have to go see Mr. Sung later. It would help if I had some information to barter with."

"I can't help you."

"We're not going to do this anymore, Sugar."

"Don't call me that."

"It's your name, Sugar. I didn't choose it."

"Neither did I."

"You and Buddy come over from China. He gets all wrapped up in tong activities, and winds up dead on my office floor. You find your way into fuck flicks. It's going to be difficult for you to come off as an innocent this time."

"Fuck you, Gold."

"Here's my problem. It doesn't take a medical degree to figure out Buddy was dead long before he showed up in my office. Sung told me yesterday that he expected Buddy to show up, 'soon' he said. That suggests Sung knew Buddy was already dead, or he would be soon. That leads to the suspicion that Sung knows who killed him. If it was just Buddy, I'd chalk the whole thing up to inscrutable oriental irony, and let it slide. Buddy wasn't the only dead guy in my office though. The other body was a friend of mine, a guy I'd known for years, and whoever smoked him thought he was doing me. That makes this personal, and I intend to get some answers."

"You don't understand anything," she said.

"Fill me in."

She waved at me with one, delicate, perfectly manicured hand. It looked like dismissal, but on the other hand she didn't tell me to leave.

I waited for her. Sometimes you just have to let these things cook.

"I have a degree," she said.

I nodded.

"I attended Kowloon University. I got a degree in biotechnology. I worked in Macau for three years, and then the fucking Chinese took over the country."

I decided, diplomatically, not to point out the fact that she was, herself, Chinese. I had learned that the Hong Kong crowd tended to distinguish themselves from the mainlanders.

"If you had any idea how poor China is... how backward. People in this country run around screaming about the Red Menace. The biggest threat to the Red Chinese, though, is the Chinese population. There are just, you know, too damn many of them. You can't command that many people, control them, if you just let them do what they want. Nobody gets to choose under the Chinese government.

"I had a degree, years of experience in my field, and they waltzed in, took over, and determined that my true calling fell elsewhere. It was humiliating. Buddy was in college when we left. He wanted to be an anthropologist. The Chinese don't value anthropology. Too many opportunities to stumble across cultural artifacts that contradict the party dogma, you know?"

"So, you came here."

"Where else could we go? Taiwan? It's just a matter of time before the mainlanders take it over, too. We had a chance to come here, and we took it. My grandfather is connected in Hong Kong, he knows people who are high up in the Triads. What did I know about the gangs? I worked in a laboratory. Grandfather came to Buddy and me, and said he had a way for us to get to America. He said he could call in some favors the Triads owed him, and we could come to San

Francisco, have a chance to make something of ourselves here."

"You didn't know the arrangement before you got here."

"We didn't know shit, Gold. Three years later, Buddy is loading and unloading trucks for a living, getting telephone calls at all hours, people telling him to be somewhere in half an hour, and he hangs up the telephone looking like someone's holding a gun on him. Three years later, and I'm on camera taking it up the ass from some piece of beef with the IQ of kitty litter, because the tongs won't let go. Sung Chow Li won't let go. We might as well be living under the goddamned Reds."

"You knew Buddy was dead when you came to me the other day."

She didn't say anything. Her eyes were moist, though, and they glistened in the last rays of the sun filtering in through the lacy window curtains. A lone tear broke loose and cut a rivulet down her cheek.

"You wanted me to confirm it for you. He'd gotten one of those telephone calls, but you knew he'd quit Sung's trucking company days before. The calls kept coming, though. People phoned to make sure he knew there was no such thing as quitting. So, he took off, told you to tell anyone who asked that he was going to a movie, but you knew it wasn't true. Then he didn't come home for days, and you knew he was dead."

"I suspected," she said. "I didn't know. I wanted to believe that I was being irrational. I wanted you to tell me that he was coming home. When you came out to Simon Wolfs' house last night and told me that Sung said he was going to show up soon, I was relieved. Then the block representative came by this afternoon and just pissed all over my life."

"You want me to find out who killed him?"

"What, hire you again?"

"I'm pretty good at this sort of thing."

"You are in so fucking way over your head, you know that, Gold?"

"Story of my life."

She looked at me for the first time since I had come in the door.

"Why?"

"I have my reasons."

"They're going to kill you."

"They can try."

"There's no *trying* with these people. You get in their way, and they'll snap you off at the knees. What happens when they find out I hired you?"

"I'm doing this with you or without you, Sugar."

She stood and walked over to me. She stood right in front of me.

"You keep calling me that name," she said. "Like you saw me at Simon's last night, and Wei Ma Lo died for you. Maybe you want a little Sugar, huh, Gold?"

She did something wiggly, like a half shrug, and the silk pajamas floated to the floor. She stood in front of me, totally naked, her bald vulva hanging in front of my face.

"You liked watching Sugar Wei last night, Joe?" she said, reaching down to caress my face. "You think maybe you'd like to help the poor girl out, maybe get some of the sweet stuff?"

"Stop," I said.

She half-turned and slid down onto my lap. She felt like she weighed all of ninety pounds. She pressed her lips against mine, and they parted a little, and her tongue danced against my teeth. Then she rose up a little, and her breasts slid up my neck and across my face.

"How shall I pay the big tough detective?" she asked. "What do you want in return for being the hero?"

Part of me made it clear that I wanted her. I couldn't control that, and she knew it. She reached down and grabbed at the crotch of my pants.

"Big brass ones," she said. "No wonder you're so brave. Can they stop bullets, Mr. Detective?"

I grabbed her by the waist, lifted her off me, and tossed her back on the sofa. As soon as she was off my lap, I stood and gazed down at her.

"You've got this all wrong," I said. "I came here to help, sure, but I also want whoever killed your brother, because they also killed my friend Benny, and they want to kill me. This isn't some cheap dime store thriller, it's real, and the stakes are just as real."

"You're going to die," she said.

"So are you. I'm not doing it on their terms, though. I'm not going to wait for them to come to me. Get dressed."

"Why?"

"I came here for information. Who's your tong block representative?"

"Albert Chang."

"Call him."

"What for?"

"I need to talk with him."

———

It took a few minutes of persuasion, but in the end Sugar called Al Chang. I was surprised how quickly he got to her door. Maybe he was already in the neighborhood collecting the skim from the local shop owners.

He knocked on Sugar's door. I stepped to the hinge side of the jam and pulled the Browning from my belt. I motioned with it for Sugar to open the door.

She unlocked the door and pulled it open. She said something in Mandarin to Chang, and he said something back, and then he walked into the room.

As soon as he closed the door, he saw me standing there with the Browning pointed between his eyes.

"What the fuck?"

"Have a seat, Albert," I said.

"What is this?"

I shoved him down on the couch.

"Let's get this straight," I said. "When I say to sit down, I mean sit. If I tell you to stand, you'd better jump up."

He turned to Sugar Wei and said something I didn't understand. I screwed the barrel of the Browning into his right ear. He didn't flinch. He did, on the other hand, stop talking to Sugar.

"Okay, I'm going to ask you the easy questions first," I said. "You came here about an hour ago to tell Sugar that her brother was dead?"

He nodded.

"Yes."

"That means someone sent you."

"Yes."

"Who sent you?"

"One of the other block representatives."

"What's his name?"

"Why do you want to know?"

I put some pressure on the Browning.

"You don't answer questions with questions, Albert. What's his name?"

"Chuck Loo."

"Bullshit. Chuck Loo works for Sung Moving."

"Yes. And he is the representative for the block where Sung Moving is located."

"Last I heard, Chuck Loo was out of town, doing a job for Mr. Sung."

"He came back."

"When?"

"Last night."

"When did Loo tell you to come see Sugar?"

Chang blinked a couple of times.

"Maybe three hours ago."

"That doesn't play, Albert. I only identified Buddy an hour and a half ago. How in hell would Loo know he was dead an hour and a half before I told the cops?"

"How in hell would I know?"

I bopped him a quick one on the top of his head with the Browning. It wasn't hard enough to really hurt, but I bet it smarted a little.

"Again with the questions. Make a guess."

"Someone told him?"

I let that one pass, since it was, more or less, a guess.

"Or maybe he knew because he was the guy who left Buddy in my office last night."

Chang didn't say anything.

Sugar did, though.

"You think Chuck Loo killed Buddy?"

"He looks as good for it as anyone else," I said. "Loo's been missing for over a week, doing something for Sung. He blows back into town last night around the same time someone is killing my friend and dumping Buddy's body in my office. Chuck Loo doesn't know me from any other roundeyes. He probably figured that when he killed Benny, he had actually gotten me. Maybe he was watching the office, waited until the owner of the gallery downstairs found the bodies, and decided he might as well inform the family. It wasn't very bright, but then I haven't run across many crooks in my life that were candidates for Fulbrights."

I pulled my phone from my jacket pocket, and dialed Frank Raymond's cell phone number. He answered on the second ring.

"Raymond."

"This is Gold. I've been talking with one of Sung Chow Li's block reps. He says Chuck Loo told him three hours ago that Buddy Wei was dead."

"How in hell could he have known that?"

"Everyone seems to be asking the same question."

"Where's Loo now?"

I still had the Browning in Albert Chang's ear. I pressed the receiver against my shoulder to muffle the sound.

"Where's Loo?"

"Probably over on his block. It's collection day."

I told Frank he might find Loo in the vicinity of Sung Moving.

"...And another thing, Frank. Remember, I told you last night, Sung told me that Loo was doing a job for him down in Los Angeles. The girl from Sung Moving told me that Loo disappeared the day that Taylor Chu was kidnapped from his office. He was in the L.A. area when all those Chinese immigrants were killed in the shipping container in Long Beach."

"Loo's beginning to sound like a bad mother. Where are you?"

"I'd rather not tell you right now. Call me back at my cell phone number when you get something out of Loo, okay?"

I gave him the number and hit the END button.

"Okay, campers," I said, crossing the room to a wingback chair covered with a shawl, "Let's all settle in. This may take a while."

"What is this?" Chang said. "Do you really mean to keep me here at gunpoint?"

"Yes. You were born over here, weren't you?"

"In San Jose. My parents came over shortly after the Communist revolution. What's that got to do with anything?"

"We may be here for some time. I just wanted to keep the conversation from going stale. Don't suppose you happen to know who Sung's grass sandal is, do you?"

Chang stiffened for a moment, as if I'd bounced a brick off his chest.

"You don't talk about things like that," he said.

"Maybe you don't," I said, "but it's been a popular topic among the round-eyed detective set lately. You can send a message up the line for me, Chang. Someone wants to squib one of the grass sandals and start a range war. This should concern you. It should really concern Sung's grass sandal."

I turned to Sugar Wei, who had not bothered to change clothes. She sat on the opposite end of the couch from Chang, staring coolly at me. I couldn't tell whether the look was admiration or contempt.

I didn't really care.

SIXTEEN

Frank Raymond called about an hour and a half later.

"We got Chuck Loo."

"How does he look for killing Benny Horowitz?"

"On an entirely subjective level, he looks peachy. On the other hand, he only had time to give us a really decent alibi before he lawyered up."

"Now, how do you suppose that happened?"

"Hell, you tell me, Gold. He's *your* lawyer."

"What?"

"We started questioning Loo, and about ten minutes later, who do you suppose walked in the door, tossing around a bunch of courthouse Latin and telling Loo to keep it zipped?"

"Louis Gai?"

"Yeah."

"Who called him?"

"Damned if I know. It wasn't Loo, though."

"He didn't get his phone call?"

"He didn't request it and we didn't offer. He was mirandized and everything, but it was like he expected to see Gai show up."

"Who is Gai, anyway? Superman? How in hell does he know to show up?"

"He told you that Sung sent him to your house, and that meant Sung had to know that Taylor Chu was dead. Question is, when did Sung know it?"

"And when did Sung know that Loo was going to be picked up?"

"What are you inferring, Gold?"

"I arrived at my Montara house with James Hong, and we called the cops. Less than an hour later, Gai pulls into the driveway. I call you and advise you the Chuck Loo looks good for killing Benny, and less than an hour later Gai shows up at the station house."

"You're burning a lot of credit, here, Eamon. I don't like what you're implying."

"It wouldn't be the first time the tongs had someone inside the police force. You know how it goes. You put people in their organization, they put people in yours. It's all about mutually assured destruction. Everyone knows what everyone else is doing, so there're no surprises."

"I hate the idea of a dirty cop."

"Doesn't change the reality. Did Gai spring Loo?"

"We didn't have anything substantial to hold him on. Like I said, his alibi was pretty firm."

"Where was he?"

"Coroner tentatively put the time of death for Benny at between seven and nine last night. Loo said he got back from L.A. around six, went straight to the trucking place, and spent the next seven hours banging that dingy receptionist chick in the back room."

"And she confirms it?"

"Yeah, she backs him up."

"You believe her?"

"Does it matter?"

"Seven hours. That's some impressive screwing."

"Oh, to be young again."

"I suppose you put a tail on Loo?"

"Natch. He made us in about three minutes, but what's he gonna do? Speaking of which, what are *you* going to do?"

I glanced at Sugar and Albert Chang. I had to be careful what I said from this point on. I didn't give a damn what Chang knew about Chuck Loo.

"You remember that butt buddy arrangement we ran across last night?" I said.

"Sure."

"Now that the party of the first part is short one attorney, I wonder who's going to handle the partnerships."

"You think Gai might have a setup with another lawyer?"

"Someone has to keep the money coming in. I think I might pay a visit to our restaurant pal, find out how he's bearing up under his loss."

"You be careful, Eamon. What's going on between Fong and Gates is none of my concern, but if Gai's mixed up in it, you can bet that Sung's hanging around in the wings."

"Another thing," I told Frank, after giving him Sugar's address, "I have a guy here who's a material witness in the murder of Benny Horowitz. Name's Albert Chang. He's a block representative for the Sung Chow Li tong. It's a sure bet he's going to go running to Sung the minute I leave the apartment. You might want to get one of the Chinatown beat cops to come over and babysit him until you can bring him in for questioning."

I hit the END button, and then dialed Heidi's number. Chang sat on the couch, staring down the barrel of the Browning, and fumed. The telephone on Heidi's end rang five times, and then the machine picked up.

"This is Eamon," I said. "I was just checking on you. I'll call you later."

I folded the phone, and placed it back in my pocket.

"Okay, Chang, I'm finished with you," I said. "I have some errands to run. No hard feelings, right?"

Chang just glared at me.

"Are you okay, Sugar?" I asked.

She nodded, but didn't say anything.

"You call Frank Raymond at the Embarcadero station," I told her. "He'll tell you how to go about claiming Buddy's body." I gave her the number. She didn't write it down.

Putting that college education to work, I guess.

"If you want it, there's a check for Buddy at Sung Moving. It's not much, just a few hundred, but it might come in handy. Also, he had about two thousand in a retirement fund."

I stowed the Browning on my belt, zipped up my jacket, and let myself out.

I hadn't gone four steps before I heard loud Mandarin shouting coming from inside Sugar's apartment. Several seconds later, I heard a slap, and a brief cry.

I wondered who slapped whom, but I didn't waste a lot of thought on it, as I passed a uniform cop heading up the stairs past me.

Like the guy in the movie said, forget it. It's Chinatown.

SEVENTEEN

Sherman Fong had three restaurants scattered around the city, but I found him on the second try. He was at the Hang Sun Palace on Stockton. I asked for him at the counter and was told to wait.

He emerged from a door at the back of the restaurant about ten minutes later. He was short, maybe five-five, and balding, with a thick salt and pepper moustache. I had expected him to be in a suit, but he walked toward me wearing khakis, and a button-down oxford cloth shirt with open collar and the sleeves rolled once or twice.

"Can I help you?" he asked.

"Eamon Gold," I said, handing him my card.

He stared at it for a moment, then reached into his shirt pocket and took out a pair of magnifying reading glasses. He put them on and stared at the card again.

"A private investigator?"

"Yes sir."

"I don't understand."

"Is there some place we can talk privately?" I asked.

He seemed a little nervous, but after a few seconds he nodded and gestured toward the door from which he had come.

"Please. Let's talk in my office."

I followed him through the restaurant to his office, which proved to be little more than a cubby. There was a formica-topped desk and a couple of chairs, a cork bulletin board, an OSHA poster in three languages. No windows. For a high roller, Fong worked in a dump.

I sat in one of the wooden chairs across from his desk. He sat in his own seat behind the desk and picked up the telephone.

"Please, no calls for about ten minutes," he said, and racked the receiver.

Okay, so I was being granted ten minutes.

"How can I help you, Mr. Gold?" he asked.

"Part of my work involves doing background checks and gathering information for attorneys around town. One of the attorneys I worked for was Taylor Chu."

He nodded. Then he pointed a thin, bony finger at me.

"Yes. I remember now. I read about it in the paper. Taylor was killed in your home."

"That's right."

"And were you somehow involved in the work Taylor did for me?"

"Um, not directly," I said. "Before his death, we discussed some of his cases, trying to figure out who had kidnapped him last week. Your name came up. As it happens, I ran into Barney Gates while working another case last night. He was concerned that I might have been investigating him in connection with the deal you two are developing."

"Yes, Mr. Gates left me a message earlier today. He seemed a little upset."

"I assured him that I wasn't checking him out. However, I have a lot of loose ends to tie up - stuff Mr. Chu had me working on before he died. I was going through some files last night, and I found some interesting - um - patterns. They suggest some irregularities in Mr. Chu's dealings with you, and I thought you would want to know about them."

"Irregularities..."

"Yes. Over the last several years, Mr. Chu brokered business deals between you and various businessmen. He prepared contracts, did credit checks, that sort of thing."

"Yes."

"In a very large number of those cases, the attorney for the partners was Louis Gai."

He leaned back in his chair.

"I hadn't noticed," he said, but the concern in his eyes made it clear he had.

"May I ask, sir, whether these deals were originated by you, or brought to you by Mr. Chu?"

"Why do you want to know?"

"Because if Mr. Chu brought them to you, it appears that he may have been engaged in some gray area dealings with Mr. Gai. In that case, I figured you would want to know."

"I don't follow."

"It's a kind of sweetheart deal. Let's say that Mr. Gai meets a businessman at a party, who indicates that he's looking at expanding his horizons. Maybe he hasn't really considered the kind of business you're doing. Gai suggests, innocently enough, that he might know someone looking for a partner to help fund a new venture. If he gets a good response, he could contact Taylor Chu, who would contact you, suggesting that he may know someone who's interested in sinking some money into a new project. Then he sells you on the project, and the rest is paperwork. Your business expands, the other guy's business expands, Gai and Chu make a ton in legal fees, everybody's happy."

"Is there something illegal about such an arrangement?" Fong asked.

"Not at all. Happens all the time. On the other hand, if Gai and Chu had a prior arrangement to set up such...

collaborations, it begins to look a little like, well, exploitation."

Fong placed his hands on the desk, palms down. He blinked a couple of times, and then nodded.

"I see what you mean. It would be as if they were on the lookout for—what do you call it?—pigeons."

"Pigeons. Exactly. It's not a con game, in the strictest sense. On the other hand, it does look as if they were working together to generate business where none existed before. Not exactly the kind of thing attorneys get a good reputation for, if it gets out."

"If it gets out," he echoed. "Is that why you're here, Mr. Gold? You want to assure that this information doesn't get out?"

Jesus. He thought I was trying to shake him down.

"No!" I said, quickly. "I think I've given you the wrong impression. Look, Mr. Fong, it's been a tough week. I've lost an employer, and a good friend of mine was killed last night in my office over near Hyde Pier. Both cases appear to be related, and both seem tied to something going on in Chinatown. Part of my job is to talk to a lot of people, and ask a lot of questions, and wait for something useful to pop up. Mr. Gai's been popping up a lot lately. I was just wondering - I know it's only been a couple of days since Taylor died, but have you made arrangements for another attorney?"

"Yes," he said.

I waited for a few seconds. It became clear he didn't want to volunteer the information.

"May I ask, sir? Is your new attorney Louis Gai?"

Fong stood behind his desk and extended his hand.

"I want to thank you for bringing this information to me," he said.

I took his hand.

"It's Gai, isn't it?" I asked.

I didn't let his hand go.

He glanced down at our clasped paws.

"I have a business to run," he said, nervously.

"Just tell me," I said. I tried to keep my voice cool, but my mouth was arid and cottony.

"I must ask you to leave now."

I stared him down for about ten seconds, and then I let his hand go.

"Thank you, Mr. Fong," I said. "I appreciate you giving me your time."

"Please go," he said.

I reached for the doorknob, walked back into the restaurant.

At the front desk, Sung's muscle Chan was chatting up the girl at the cash register, but his eyes were locked in my direction.

He didn't look happy.

Now I knew why it had taken Sherman Fong ten minutes to come out to greet me. He had been occupied sending up a red flag to Sung.

Curiouser and curiouser.

I considered finding a back way out of the restaurant, then decided that this was exactly what Chan wanted me to do. They probably had a car waiting out back for me, or maybe just a couple of kung fu experts with bad attitudes.

I walked toward the register. Chan watched me the way a cobra watches a mongoose.

"Boy, am I glad to see you!" I said as I reached him, extending my hand in the universal gesture of good will.

It's an automatic thing, taking someone's offered hand. It's something you don't normally think about.

Maybe Chan should have thought about it.

He took my right hand. With my left, I grabbed the Sig Sauer from his shoulder holster, flicked the safety, and held it against his side under his jacket.

"Let's take a walk," I said, gesturing toward the door with my chin. I tried to keep the cheerful bounce in my voice, but it still came out thin and stressed.

"You don't know what you're doing," Chan said.

"Damned right about that," I said. "Let's go."

I walked him out the front door of the restaurant.

EIGHTEEN

As we left the Hang Sun Palace, I tossed my free arm around Chan's shoulders, and forced a smile onto my face.

"Where are they?" I asked, through clenched teeth.

"Who?"

"You didn't come here alone. You had help. Where are they?"

"Behind the restaurant."

Goodie. I had guessed correctly. Kewpie doll for Eamon.

I steered Chan toward the Caddie, which I had parked across the street from the restaurant.

"We're going for a ride," I said. "Ever drive a Caddie?"

"I drive a Mercedes."

"Be a good boy, and maybe you'll get to drive it again, understand?" I said, punching him in the side with the Sig.

He nodded, as I pulled open the door and let him slide in behind the wheel. I slipped around to the passenger side and sat next to him.

"Where to?" he asked.

Just like that. He was a cool one.

"Lincoln Park. The Baker Beach parking lot."

I handed him the keys, and he pulled away from the curb.

"First things first," I said. "Fong called Sung to complain about me barging into his business?"

"Mr. Sung's affairs are none of your fucking business, Gold."

I punched him in the kidney with the Sig again.

"Lot of dead Chinamen all over San Francisco the last several days," I said. "One more probably isn't gonna make much of a dent."

"Up yours," Chan said.

I reversed the Sig and brought the butt of the pistol down on the knuckles of his right hand, wrapped around the steering wheel. I probably didn't break them, but he wouldn't be playing the piano for a while.

He grimaced and made a sound deep in his throat. He didn't cry out, though.

"We're going to be civil," I said. "We're going to cooperate. Now let's try it again. Tong called Sung?"

"I don't know," he said. "Mr. Sung just told me to take a couple of men to Hang Sun and pick you up."

"Where were you going to take me?"

"Where do you think? To Mr. Sung."

"Well, maybe before the night's over we'll check in on him. Who's Sung's grass sandal?"

"Fuck you."

This time I did break a couple of knuckles. They started to swell up like scuppernongs as soon as I rapped them with the butt of the Sig Sauer. Chan yelped then. Some things you just can't hold in.

"Who's Sung's grass sandal?" I asked again.

"You don't understand," Chan said, gripping the wheel harder with his left hand. He started to take his right hand off the wheel.

"Keep both of them up there," I said, and raised the Sig again. Chan placed his right hand back on the wheel.

"Now, what don't I understand?" I asked.

"The grass sandal. He is a revered officer. His strength comes from his anonymity."

"Bullshit. Every shop owner in Chinatown knows who the grass sandals are."

"Yes, and they all work for the tongs. They know it is important to keep the secret."

"Why?"

"Because that is the way it has always been, damn it!"

I thought about this for a second.

"Tradition."

"Hell, yes, tradition. The structure in the tongs is centuries old. They do things now the same way they did them in the seventeenth century. We don't talk openly about tong business, especially to Westerners."

"Where does Louis Gai fit in?"

"Damn it, you keep asking the same question!"

I stopped.

"Louis Gai?" I asked. "He's the grass sandal?"

Chan shook his head.

"No. Even if he were, I'd deny it. He isn't, though. He's... he's... like in *The Godfather*, the part Robert Duvall played."

"*Consigliere*. A counselor to Mr. Sung."

"Yes."

"I thought that was the role of the grass sandal. To counsel, and mediate."

"Then you still don't understand."

Chan turned the car into the Presidio. As he did, I saw a pair of headlights swing in behind us.

"We've got a tail," I said.

Chan didn't say anything.

"Keep driving," I told him. "No sudden moves."

We drove along for half a mile, and then I saw a familiar road on the right.

"Right turn signal," I said.

He flipped the switch. In the side mirror, I saw the car behind us start to signal.

Could have been a coincidence.

"Don't turn," I said. "Just drive straight ahead."

We passed the road without turning. The signal on the tail flashed off, and it continued to follow us.

Okay. No coincidence.

That's good.

I don't trust coincidences.

A few moments later, we left the Presidio, and drove by the entrance to the Golden Gate Bridge. I was tempted to tell Chan to take the bridge across to Marin County. Maybe take a leisurely drive up through, say, Canada.

We were about to pull off the road into the parking lot at Baker Beach when the car behind us pulled up close. I held onto the Sig with my right hand and grabbed at my own Browning with my left. I mentally kicked myself for leading us into what looked like an ambush.

Just as Chan turned into the parking lot, the rear window was filled with a flashing red light, and someone beamed a high-powered searchlight into the Caddie. There was a short *whoop* behind us.

The cops.

Chan seemed to tense up.

"Okay, what do you want to do now?" he asked.

I holstered my Browning, and sat on the Sig.

"Put it in park," I said.

I pulled down the passenger visor and looked back in the mirror. It wasn't easy, with all the flashing lights. After several seconds, the driver's door opened, and a large figure stepped out. He walked over to Chan's window, and rapped on the glass.

Chan pressed the button to lower the window.

James Hong leaned down and stared into the car.

"You okay, Gold?" he asked.

"Peachy," I said. "Have you been following me all day?"

"Most of it. What have we here?" he said, grabbing Chan's chin and pulling his face around to look at it.

Chan let his head be turned. He didn't like it much.

Hong said something to him in Mandarin.

Chan didn't reply.

"Your pal seems to have left his green card somewhere else," Hong told me. "That presents a problem for me."

"His name's Chan," I said. "I don't know his first name. He works for Sung Chow Li."

"Muscle?"

"Yeah. He tried to waylay me at Hang Sun Palace."

Hong nodded.

"I don't suppose you waylay easily," he said. "You have any more business with Mr. Chan tonight?"

"He wants to take me to see Mr. Sung."

"Sounds like a one-way trip."

"That's the way I read it."

Hong opened the door, took Chan by the elbow, and led him back to the Homeland Security car behind the Caddie. After depositing Chan in the back seat, he spoke with his partner for a couple of moments. His partner slid over behind the wheel, and the flashers cut off. Hong shut the door and the Homeland Security car started to pull around to leave the parking lot.

Seconds later, Hong lowered himself into the Caddy and buckled the seatbelt.

"I always wanted to drive one of these," he said.

"What's the play?"

"I figure Sung won't zip you while you're accompanied by a government agent. I'm kind of interested in what he has to tell you."

NINETEEN

"Why were you following me?" I asked, as Hong turned the Caddy onto Ashbury.

"The kid who got killed on your floor last night was an illegal," he said. "That made it my business. Since whoever killed him thought he was also killing you instead of your friend, I had a feeling they'd keep trying."

"You know who killed them?"

"No. I have a hunch, though."

"What's your hunch?"

"I think," he said, smiling slyly. "it involves something happening down in Chinatown."

"No shit? Never would have occurred to me. You Feds are something else, you know that?"

We drove along for several minutes, until an idea came to me.

"Hey, James, let's make a detour."

"Where to?"

"I want to drop by Sung Moving before we go visit the boss."

He turned left onto Grant, and several minutes later we parked outside the building near North Beach.

"How are you going to get in?" Hong asked.

I tapped the side of my head.

"Just watch."

I stepped out of the Caddy and walked up to the front door.

Then I rang the bell.

Through the dirty glass of the front window, I could see a light in the very back, and a figure crossed in front of it. Several seconds later, a door in the back of the building opened and a male profile started walking toward the front door.

He opened it and stared out at me.

"What the fuck?" he asked.

I pulled the Browning out and placed the barrel right between his eyes.

"*This* the fuck. Are you Chuck Loo?"

His eyes rolled up and tried to focus on the gun. He nodded, slowly.

"I'm coming in, Chuck."

He nodded again and started to back up. I followed him inside and closed the door behind us.

"Is the girl here?" I asked.

"No. I sent her home."

"We're alone?" I said, accenting it by poking the gun into this forehead to let him know it would be a bad thing to lie.

"Just you and me," he said.

I gestured for him to go to the back of the building and followed him there.

My nose wrinkled as we entered his quarters. There was a sour, dank odor that was about fifty percent human, and fifty percent rot. Chuckie had a mattress lying in the corner, covered with stained sheets and a thin blanket. There were a couple of chairs, and a small dresser with a cracked mirror.

I told Chuck Loo to sit in one of the chairs. I sat in the other and kept the Browning pointed at him.

"Chan's not going to be around anymore," I said. I didn't bother telling him it was because Chan was going to be deported. I figured he'd be more cooperative if he thought I'd zagged Sung's bodyguard.

He nodded.

"Before he left, he told me some things. I want you to confirm them. Do you understand?"

He stared at me.

"I want you to tell me if what he said is true."

"Okay," Loo said.

"If you lie to me, I'll know. I don't like it when people lie to me."

"Okay."

"You were in Long Beach last week with Lanny Gow and Sammy Chin."

I let it hang there.

"Yeah," he said.

"You three met the *Xinhua Voyager* there."

"That's right."

"The three of you opened a container there and machine-gunned thirty-seven Chinese nationals."

"What about it?"

"Why?"

"Huh?"

"You work for Sung Chow Li. The container was shipped to Sung. Presumably, he imported the thirty-seven soldiers as part of a plan to take over all the operations in Chinatown. Why kill your own guys?"

He stared at me.

"Can I smoke?" he asked.

"No fast moves."

He reached into the pocket of his robe and pulled out a pack of Winstons with a matchbook stuck in the cellophane. He shook out a cigarette and stuck it in his mouth and lit it.

He blew a cloud of smoke into the air, and pointed at me, the cigarette smoldering in his hand.

"You don't know shit. Who in hell are you anyway?"

I ignored the question.

"You weren't really balling your secretary for seven hours last night, were you?"

"You been talking to the cops?"

I bopped him over the bridge of the nose with the pistol. It broke the skin, and blood oozed from the wound. He dropped the cigarette and grabbed his face with both hands. I ground out the cigarette with the heel of my shoe.

"Ow! Damn, man!"

"You weren't really with the girl all last evening," I said.

"No! Shit, man, I think you broke my nose!"

"Who killed Buddy Wei? You, Chin, or Gow?"

"Lanny did that."

"But he didn't do it in Eamon Gold's office. He did it somewhere else, and then took him there."

"Lanny killed him in the back of one of the trucks, on the interstate."

"Why?"

"Buddy tried to cut out on us. He quit his job at Sung Moving and tried to make a run for New York. Thought maybe he could disappear there."

"You caught up with him?"

"It was easy. We knew he was about to bolt, so we just waited for him to leave that apartment he shared with his sister. We picked him up a block away."

"That was over a week ago. He wasn't dead twenty-four hours when he was found this morning."

Chuck rubbed his nose gingerly.

"And?"

"Where did you keep him all that time?"

"We have a place. Over in Alameda. It's in an industrial park."

"That's where you kept Taylor Chu?"

Finally, I had surprised him.

"Yeah. How'd you know...?"

"I'll ask the questions. Who killed Chong Lin Kow?"

"I did. That was personal. He kicked the shit out of me while I was stoned. I couldn't let that ride, man."

"Are you legal?"

"Born right here in Chinatown, over on Pacific. Why?"

"You weren't brought here by Sung's Snakeheads?"

"No. Is this going somewhere?"

"One more question. Who killed the other guy in my office?"

Shit.

I'd screwed up.

"Your office?" he said. "You're Gold?"

"Why'd you kill the guys in the container in Long Beach?"

"Chan didn't tell you this shit," Loo said. "This is bullshit."

I stood, walked over to him, and pressed the Browning into his forehead again.

"The other dead guy in my office was a friend of mine. Whoever killed him got the wrong guy. You really don't want to be the one who killed him. Understand?"

"I ain't talkin' no more, and you ain't gonna shoot me."

"Don't be so certain. I'm pretty stressed. I might act out of character."

To illustrate my point, I lowered the Browning and pumped a round into the floor between his feet. The explosion rang like a mortar shell in the small room. He jumped. The chair fell over backward, and his head rapped against the floor. I stepped around and pointed the gun down at his head.

"Here's how I see it," I said. "You're Sung's block manager, but you're also working for someone else. The container in Long Beach really was intended for Sung, and when you and your two buddies intercepted it you were doing it for another party. Who turned you? The Hop Sing?"

"You'd better just pull the trigger, big man, because I'm as good as dead if I tell you."

For a second, I actually considered it.

Chuck Loo may not have killed Benny Horowitz, but it was a slam-dunk that he was in on the job. I stood over him, my finger caressing the trigger of the Browning, trying to decide on which side of grace it was going to fall.

Seconds later, someone grasped my elbow and pulled the barrel away from Loo's head.

"Put it away," Hong said. "We have company."

I safetied the pistol just as Frank Raymond and Dexter Spears walked through the door, flanked by a couple of plainclothes cops I didn't know.

"Okay, Gold, you want to explain what you're doing fucking up my stakeout?"

"Some fuckin' stakeout," Loo said, as he rolled over to get to his feet.

"I figured Loo lied to you. I just wanted to give him a shot at clearing the record," I said.

"You are way out of line, here," Frank told me. "Give Spears your gun."

I eyed Frank's partner.

"Like hell I will."

"I'd hate to have to cuff you and take you downtown," Frank said.

"That won't be necessary," Hong said, breaking in.

"Who in hell are you?" Frank asked.

Hong pulled out his government ID card.

"Hong. James Hong. Homeland Security."

"Bet you really love saying that," Frank said.

"Mr. Gold is assisting me with an investigation into the murder of Buddy Wei."

"Bullshit," Spears said. "That's an SFPD case."

"Wei was an illegal. That makes it my case, too. If he was killed by other illegals, we want to know."

"Well, fuck me," Frank said, throwing up his hands. "And since when do the Feds allow some burnout private dick to toss in with them? This stinks."

"Inspector," Hong said. "I think we can all work together on this thing. As it happens, I think Mr. Gold was able to find some information from Mr. Loo here that may be material to both our cases."

"Bullshit," Loo said, holding his nose. "Asshole forced his way in here and beat me up. I didn't tell him shit, and even if I did it can't be used against me. Fucker held a gun on me. That's coercion. I might even charge him with assault."

"Just what did you tell him, Loo?" Frank asked.

"Not a thing. You guys are harassing me. I want you out of my place."

I reached into my jacket pocket and pulled out a pocket dictation recorder.

"It's all here," I said. "Chuck told me that Lanny Gow killed Buddy Wei, but he didn't tell me who killed Benny Horowitz. Chuck here killed Chong Kow on the road to Long Beach. He also admitted taking part in the killing of those thirty-seven Chinese nationals on the docks at Long Beach."

I played a couple of minutes of the tape for Frank and Spears.

"Were you holding a gun on him at the time, Eamon?" Frank asked.

"Yeah, I was."

"Then it's not admissible. You know that."

"Doesn't matter," I said. "I wasn't planning on using it in court. Before Agent Hong and I came here, we were on the way to visit Sung Chow Li. It occurred to me that we ought to come bearing gifts. You're never going to pin Benny's killing on Chuckie here, because he'll just drag that twist of his into court to alibi him out. Twenty-four hours from now, Lanny Gow and Sammy Chin will be rancid memories, unless you put them under protection immediately. Maybe you can talk one of them into turning on the others, but I doubt it. These guys are scared shitless of someone. This thing just isn't going to fly in court. Where I'm going, they don't give much of a damn about rules of evidence."

I stowed the Browning in my shoulder holster and walked out the door. James Hong followed me.

I half expected Frank to try to hold me up. Deep down, though, I knew he agreed with me. He didn't have a case against Chuck Loo, and he never would.

TWENTY

"You're going to pay for that, you know," Hong told me as we drove down Columbus.

"What?"

"You don't rub a cop's face in shit and walk away. He's gonna fuck up your whole week."

"Frank understands the situation," I said. "He didn't like me pointing out the obvious. Once he cut Loo back onto the streets, the kid was terminal anyway. I boosted another block manager earlier in the evening, guy named Albert Chang. By now, he's already lawyered up and he's gone running back to Sung. There's gonna be blood running in the gutters down in Chinatown, and it's coming soon."

"This shit about Chuck working for someone else?"

"Yeah. Something hinky's about to cut loose among the tongs. I'm reasonably certain that Sung wasn't behind the killings in Long Beach, but I do suspect that he was the one who hired Chong Kow and brought him out to the left coast to do a little wet work. The only thing I don't know is who Kow was hired to kill. It had to be one of the grass sandals, but I don't know who they are."

"Is that all?"

I turned to him.

"What do you mean?"

Hong pointed to his face.

"Look at me. Where do I come from?"

"You know who the grass sandals are?"

"Of course. You met with one of them tonight."

"Fong?"

"Fong is Sung's grass sandal."

I thought about it for a second.

"Of course. That makes sense, now. Taylor Chu was his attorney, taking care of all his legal matters, writing his contracts. Sung told me that Taylor Chu was on the road to becoming a grass sandal. Fong was training him, showing him the ropes."

"That's the way they do things. Master and student. All that *Snatch-The-Pebble-From-My-Hand-Grasshopper* shit."

"Well, Kow wasn't here to kill Fong. Why would Sung want to kill his own grass sandal?"

"Doesn't seem to make sense, does it?"

"Nothing much has in the last week. Can you put together a list of the grass sandals working Chinatown?"

"I suppose. Why?"

"If Fong wasn't the target, then one of the others was. If we can find out which one, I'll bet that's the tong that turned Chuck Loo and his buds."

"Gold, this doesn't play. The pieces aren't fitting together."

"What am I missing?"

"You told me earlier that Sung had sent Chuck Loo, Lanny Gow, and Sammy Chin on a delivery. That's what he told you. Now, it looks as if they went to Long Beach to massacre the guys in the shipping container. There's no way they could do that and get away with it, unless Sung approved it."

"What are you suggesting?"

204   *Richard Helms*

"That you have it backward. Sung did send his dickheads to Long Beach, specifically to intercept the shipping container."

"That means he was killing his own soldiers."

"Maybe he had to."

"I don't get it."

"Maybe it was an appeasement. One of the other Dragon Heads found out that Sung had hired some nasty talent from Hong Kong – Kow -- *and* that he had a battalion of heavily armed soldiers coming into the docks at Long Beach. They arranged to kidnap Taylor Chu as a warning. They dropped the fake Chu off the bridge to show what would happen if Sung didn't fall into line. They demanded that the soldiers be neutralized and that Sung call off his hit man as their price for returning Chu and…"

"And Sung wanted Chu safe, because he was being groomed to take Sherman Fong's place as Sung's grass sandal," I added. "So, he sent the Sung Moving Chuckleheads to do *two* jobs. They pulled off the massacre in Long Beach, and on the way back they eliminated Chong Kow. That fits so far. There's just one hitch. When Chuck Loo told me about the place they took Buddy Wei in Alameda, I mentioned that he had also taken Taylor there. Chuck nearly shit his pants. He figured I'd found out he kidnapped Chu."

"You were right the first time, about Chuck Loo working both sides of the street."

"That means there's a player here we don't have a score card for."

"Yeah. And it's the ones you don't see coming that hurt you the most."

We parked the Caddy about a block down the street from Sung's office and trudged up Grant Avenue to visit him.

Once inside the building, Hong's badge got us through three levels of interceptors. After waiting a few minutes, we were ushered into Sung's inner office.

He was waiting for us this time.

"Mr. Gold," he said. "Agent Hong."

I turned to Hong.

"You've met?"

He nodded, his jaw set firmly in a grimace.

"We've met."

"Indeed," Sung said. "Have a seat, gentlemen. Can I have some drinks brought up for you?"

"Nothing for me," I said. Actually, I was dying for a beer, but I figured I'd want all my wits about me, and both hands free for the foreseeable future.

"I'm fine," Hong said.

"Mr. Chan didn't bring you," Sung said to me.

"He's in the custody of the INS," I said. "He tried to pick me up at Fong's restaurant. He didn't do a very good job of it."

"So Mr. Fong informed me. He told me about your conversation this evening, after you left. He told me your... very *interesting* theory about Taylor Chu and Louis Gai."

"And Mr. Fong informed me that Gai serves you in a very close, confidential way."

"So he does."

"Fong was training Taylor Chu to be the next Sung Chow Li grass sandal, wasn't he?"

"I've already confirmed our plans. Are you still investigating the Taylor Chu killing, Mr. Gold? I thought we had an... arrangement."

"We did. As it happens, I know who killed just about everyone *but* Chu. My concern now is who killed Benny

Horowitz in my office last night, and left Buddy Wei's body lying next to him."

"Besides the obvious invasion of your privacy, why are you looking into this?"

"Because whoever did it meant to kill me, that's why. I'm on somebody's hit list, and I'm here to make very certain it isn't yours."

The door to Sung's office opened, and I instinctively reached under my jacket for the Browning. I turned to see a young girl, maybe twenty, carrying a tray with a porcelain teapot and two cups, enter the room.

She set the tray on Sung's desk and poured a single cup of tea. He thanked her, and she left the way she had come.

"Please allow me to assure you," Sung said, as he stirred his tea. "I have no intention of killing you, Mr. Gold, however irritating you have become."

"Tell me," I said, "With Taylor Chu dead, who's next in line to replace Fong as grass sandal?"

"I'm sorry, but I don't see that as pertinent. Are you certain you won't have some tea?"

"It occurs to me that the next guy in line would have a pretty big motive, don't you think?"

"If he knew he were a candidate, of course," Sung agreed. "Unfortunately, it doesn't work that way in our organization. There's no clearly defined line of succession, if you will."

"Louis Gai didn't waste any time cozying up to Fong after Chu was killed."

"What are you suggesting?"

I pulled the tape recorder from my jacket pocket and played the tape of my interview with Chuckie Loo.

"Here's the way I see it," I said. "Buddy Wei was incidental. He was a convenient chump, a warm expendable body. When he decided to take his act on the road, his value to you dropped to practically nothing. Loo, Chin, and Gow had to take care of business in Long Beach, so you could get Taylor Chu back from whoever had kidnapped him. You didn't want to lose your future grass sandal, after all.

"On the other hand, your three musketeers had a separate agenda. Several days ago, after Chu was released, when I had him holed up at my house in Montara, I was tailed by three Hop Sing Tong gun monkeys. One of them told me that they were looking for Taylor Chu. That means they didn't have a clue where he was, but he was killed later that same day. So, we can eliminate your competition at Hop Sing.

"Someone else, though, put a homing device on my car, and that's what led them to Chu at my beach house. Again, this eliminates the Hop Sing. If they planted the device, there was no reason to tail me.

"Okay, so it could have been one of the other remaining tongs. On the other hand, I haven't heard a peep from them since this whole thing began. That's strange.

"So, here's my scenario. You tell me if it's out of line. The Hop Sing discovered you were bringing in thirty-seven armed Chinese soldiers from Hong Kong, in a shipping container on the *Xinhua Voyager*. They kidnapped Taylor Chu and let you know if those soldiers left the shipyard, Chu would be killed. You had to send Chuck Loo, Lanny Chin, and Sammy Gow to Long Beach to intercept the shipping container. I have Chuck Loo admitting to that on this tape. On the way back, Chuck Loo took care of some personal business when he killed Chong Lin Kow, retribution for the butt-kicking Chong had delivered to him at the raver. This was fortunate, because Chong had been imported, by you, to kill one of the other grass sandals to destabilize the tong structures just enough to allow your covert army to take over the whole Chinatown tong scene. You realized, if Chong completed his assignment, you'd have wasted your own soldiers for nothing. So, Chong had to die.

"That left Taylor Chu, your grass sandal-in-training, floating around somewhere, and you didn't know where. That's why you pulled me in the first time, so that I could get a message to him letting him know that you weren't involved in his kidnapping, that it was safe for him to come back in."

"There's a third party operating here, though, someone we haven't identified. Someone – not you, not the Hop Sing – wired my car with the homing device. That same entity killed Taylor Chu and made everything that had happened up to that point worthless.

"And then there's the problem of Chuckie Loo's tacit admission on this tape that he, Chin, and Gow were involved in the original kidnapping of Taylor Chu. That means you have a serious breach of security, Mr. Sung. Some of your guys are playing both sides of some fence. The question is, whose team is on the other side?"

Sung sat very still, absorbing what I had told him. He turned to Hong.

"You can leave us now, Mr. Hong."

"Yes sir," Hong said, and stood up. Before leaving, he turned to me. "Don't worry, Eamon. He won't hurt you while I'm around. Mr. Sung wants to tell you some things he knows I can't hear."

He turned to Sung.

"Mr. Sung, I'm sorry for having to bust Chan. Business is business, though, right?"

"Of course," Sung said. "Thank you for apologizing."

"I'll wait for you downstairs," Hong told me, and then he walked out of the room.

"I'm troubled by what you've told me," Sung said, as he put the teacup back onto the tray. "First of all, please let me assure you that I did not arrange for Mr. Wei's body to be left in your office, or for you to be killed in the process. I heard about that incident only this morning."

"From Albert Chang."

"Yes. Mr. Chang was informed, I am told, by Mr. Loo."

"Who knew that Buddy Wei was dead before Wei was even identified. Of course, Loo knew this because he was in on Wei's killing."

"Which I did not authorize. You understand, of course, that what I'm telling you now is in confidence."

"You're saying that you didn't authorize a killing that, *of course*, you have no power to order. Since, *of course*, you're just a simple businessman."

"Something like that," he said, smiling for the first time since I had entered the room. "It's clear to me, now, that some of my employees are also working for someone else. Unfortunately, I have about as much idea who they are as you do. I will confirm several things you have suggested.

"First, I did not kidnap Taylor Chu. Second, I was required to make certain… adjustments to my plans in order to secure his release. Third, I did not authorize a homing device to be placed on your car. Fourth, I did not know that Mr. Loo killed Chong Lin Kow. Finally, as I have already told you, I did not authorize what happened in your office last evening."

"May I ask you a couple of questions?" I said.

He didn't answer. I couldn't tell whether that meant *no*, or he was just waiting. I followed Gold's Fifth Law, which says that it's much easier to get forgiveness than permission.

"Who told you that Taylor Chu was dead?"

"That was Mr. Gai."

"How'd he find out?"

"He has a contact at the police department."

"You authorized him to represent me?"

"It was his suggestion, but I agreed."

"Why?"

"It was a good way to keep an eye on you."

"You did know that Taylor Chu and Louis Gai had a sweetheart arrangement to set up business deals in the city?"

"I was informed of this just this afternoon."

"By Mr. Fong."

"That's correct."

"Your grass sandal."

Sung just stared at me. He wasn't going to confirm that one, but Hong already had. I let it ride.

"Did you assign Gai to represent Chong Lin Kow when Chu was kidnapped?"

"I did."

"Why?"

"Because he suggested that it would be a good idea."

"In order to keep a *close eye* on Chong?"

"Yes," he said, drawing the word out.

"As your *consigliere*, Gai is privy to all kinds of information about your business, isn't he?"

"He has my confidence."

"Did he know that Taylor Chu was in line to be your next grass sandal?"

Sung didn't answer.

His eyes, however, narrowed until they were nothing but obsidian slits.

And he was no longer smiling.

TWENTY-ONE

I caught up with Hong in the lobby of Sung's building.

"Where do you want me to drop you off?" I asked.

"Who said I did?"

"I have to shake you loose, James. From here on in, you're a liability."

"You want to put that in short words, Chief?"

"No."

"You're saying you're getting ready to be involved in things I shouldn't know about?"

"Something like that."

"Hold on."

He pulled a cell phone from his jacket pocket and dialed a number.

"This is Hong. Have you processed Chan yet? Good. I need to be picked up, corner of Grant and Pacific. Fifteen minutes. Fine."

"I could have driven you somewhere," I said as we walked out the front door of the building.

"You look like a man on a mission," he said. "Don't think I should be getting in the way. Word of advice?"

"Any time."

"I think maybe you're mixed up in something where it's going to be damned hard to tell the cowboys from the Indians."

"You have a suggestion?"

"Shoot everyone. Let God sort it out."

I grinned as I grasped his extended hand.

"It's tempting," I told him. "But that would kind of confuse the issue of which side *I'm* on, wouldn't it?"

He reached into his jacket pocket and extracted a folded piece of paper. It was a sheet of Sung's stationery.

"What's this?" I asked.

"That list you wanted. Use it wisely. No shit, Eamon, that sheet of paper can do you as much ill as it can good."

"Thanks," I said, stuffing the paper in my own jacket pocket.

"See you around," Hong said. Then he turned and started the uphill walk to Pacific Avenue.

My office was still festooned with yellow crime scene tape, so I headed straight over to my house on Russian Hill.

I still didn't know who had killed Benny Horowitz in my office, but I had narrowed it down to one of the Sung Moving Stooges—Chuckie Loo, Sammy Chin, or Lanny Gow. One of them had pulled the trigger, and I still wasn't certain it had been such a hot idea not to spatter Loo's brains all over his stained rug.

On the other hand, it was a dead-bang certainty that none of them had ordered me killed. That was my real objective, because I had a feeling that when I knew who had put the button on me, I'd know who killed Taylor Chu.

I opened a bottle of Michelob and sat by my eastern window, watching the lights of the Bay Bridge and running the main points over and over in my mind.

Louis Gai looked so dirty, I couldn't help but make him the leading candidate. Somehow, he seemed to know everything that happened, almost as soon as it happened. It was a sure thing that, when questioned, he'd attribute this knowledge to a well-established crew of informants – both off and *on* the police force. The real question was, who knew what first?

The convolutions were beginning to give me a headache. I could chase my tail for the next year and not get any closer to the truth.

Maybe it was time to flush out a few of the fuzzier, less distinct faces in this game.

I placed a telephone call to Frank Raymond.

"You're wearing out your welcome Gold," he told me when he answered the phone. "I really didn't appreciate you screwing up our party tonight."

"Geez, Frank, you just did such a good job of hiding your lookouts, I never suspected they were there."

"Blow me. What do you want? I'm busy."

"It's occurred to me that whoever is running this show has a pipeline into your outfit."

"Yeah? So?"

"You don't sound surprised."

"We've already been over this. I hate dirty cops as much as you do, but there's nothing I can do about it. What am I supposed to do? Round up every Asian cop in the department and give them the third degree?"

"Who says it's an Asian cop?"

"What are you saying?"

"When I tell you something, it's like I'm wired right in to the tongs. Whoever's passing information along is close to you."

"Say what you're thinking."

"Just thought you'd like to know."

"I'll alert the press. I'm really, *really* busy, okay?"

"I think I know who's turned Chuckie Loo and the other stooges."

"Okay, I'll bite. Who?"

"No way, Frank. Every time I tell you something, it gets posted on the bulletin board in the break lounge. I've managed to turn one of the key players myself. I'm meeting him later tonight. I have about forty thousand of Sung's dollars to bargain with, get him to tell me everything."

"I don't suppose you want to tell me where this little summit is taking place?"

"Not over a non-secure phone. I'll get back with you tomorrow morning and let you know what I find out."

"Why do I get the idea you're in way over your head?"

"Must be all the bubbles. I'll call you later if I have anything you can use."

"You be careful, Eamon."

He didn't bother saying goodbye.

———

At two o'clock in the morning, I climbed into the Caddy and started driving. I looped around the Embarcadero, swung by Fisherman's Wharf, and then through the Presidio, all the while surreptitiously checking my rearview mirror for tails.

By the time I'd made the big circle around the city to Candlestick, I could make out two distinct sets of headlights behind me. Just to be certain, I made a little whoopteedoo detour through a pair of cloverleaf interchanges. The headlights dropped back, but they didn't leave my six.

Back in the city, I jumped on the ramp to the Bay Bridge, and drove across the bay to Oakland, then hopped the freeway to Alameda. I had a feeling the guys behind me knew right where I was headed, because they dropped even farther back, until I could barely tell which headlights theirs were, and which were simply fellow late-night travelers.

At Alameda I pulled off the freeway and into an industrial park, which became shabbier and shabbier until I hit a stretch of dark, oversized Quonsets. It took me a few minutes to find the address I wanted. I parked the car and walked to the rear of the former aircraft hangar, stood under a dim, crackling and buzzing mercury streetlamp.

I didn't have to wait long. I heard the crunching of tires on broken window glass, and two pairs of headlights arced around the back of the building. The cars stopped, and both drivers got out at the same time. They walked slowly toward me.

"When I'm right, I'm right," I said to them. "But when I'm wrong, boy do I miss by a mile."

"Is your contact here yet?" Frank Raymond asked.

"No. So, it's you, Frank. I expected Spears. I'm disappointed."

"Spears is stupid," Frank said. "But he's honest. Me?"

He shrugged.

Sherman Fong stood slightly behind and to one side of Raymond.

"Mr. Fong, this is also a surprise. I thought Louis Gai was coming."

"Gai was your contact? Surely you didn't expect to buy him with a mere forty thousand dollars."

"I'll try anything once. You do what you can with what you're given. I... uh, suppose I know now who the mole in the SFPD is, and who's been feeding him information. This jumbles my story a little, though."

"How so, Eamon?" Frank asked.

"I thought Louis Gai was the one who turned Chuckie Loo and his pals, got them to kidnap Taylor Chu and kill Chong Lin Kow. I figured he did it because, as Sung's *consigliere*, he knew that Chu was in line to become grass sandal, and he wanted the position for himself. That was why he cozied up to Chu, put together the sweetheart deal. Now I realize that he was being played all along, just like the rest of us."

"That's a big guess," Frank said.

"Not so big as it looks. Sung had a plan to destabilize the tongs by importing Chong to put the zotz on one of four guys."

I pulled the sheet James Hong had given me from my jacket pocket.

"Specifically, I think he planned to kill Roger Hoy, the grass sandal for the Hop Sing tong. Am I right, Mr. Fong?"

"Go on, Gold," Fong said.

"You didn't think this was such a hot idea, Mr. Fong. You figured the Hop Sing might consider retaliating, and that made you a high priority target. So, you decided to intercede in both plans, by first taking the soldiers on the *Xinhua Voyager* out of the picture by kidnapping Taylor Chu, and then by killing Chong. It was easy to convert Chuckie Loo to your side. After all, Chong had danced all over his face at the raver. It was a matter of honor for him.

"You had Chuckie Loo and his guys kidnap Chu. You couldn't know, though, that Sung would decide to send them to Long Beach to shoot up the cargo container. They couldn't do that and keep an eye on Taylor, so they had to let him go.

"So, Taylor finds his way to me, and we head off to Montara, but you didn't know that. You convinced Sung that I probably knew where Taylor was holed up, and he invited me to his office, where he gave me a message to pass on, reassuring Taylor that Sung hadn't authorized the kidnapping."

"More guesses," Fong said.

"I do have a question. I've figured out who everyone else is in this little horse opera, except for one person. Who was the body dropped off the Bay Bridge?"

"Who knows?" Frank said. "Just some illegal the Snakeheads brought over."

"Shut up," Fong said to Raymond.

"Relax," Raymond told him. "This ends tonight. Soon as Gai shows up, we'll take care of both him and Gold. Kill two birds with one stone."

"When did they turn you, Frank?" I asked.

"What? Worried that I might have been rotten when we were partners? Don't worry. I didn't get on this gravy train until I already had my gold shield."

"Gai didn't set up the sweetheart deal with Taylor Chu," I said. "You did that, didn't you, Fong? You put ideas in Gai's head, suggested that maybe being *consigliere* wasn't ambitious enough for him. You dangled the grass sandal position in front of his eyes."

"Taylor Chu was always the wrong choice for grass sandal," Fong said. "He didn't have the balls to do the really hard work. He didn't have a killer instinct."

"Not like you," I observed.

"Not at all like me."

"So you recruited Gai, convinced him that, with Chu out of the way, he'd be a certain alternative choice."

"I did nothing of the kind. Whatever reasons Gai had for cooperating with me were his own. He's a very ambitious man, Mr. Gold. He could figure out what his end was worth in this deal."

Frank Raymond walked up to me, his service piece in his hand.

"Give me your gun, Eamon."

I opened my jacket, showing him the Browning. He reached in with his free hand, jerked it from my belt, and stowed it in his jacket pocket.

"You should have just taken the money and dropped this thing," Frank said, backing away. "Sung's money could have kept you for half a year or more. Why'd you keep at it?"

"I was ready to give it up," I said. "I really was. Sung made it clear that the forty thousand was a payoff. I thought you understood that last night, at Chu's office. What I can't figure is why someone tried to squib me in my office."

"It was convenient," Fong said. "You kept nosing around Chuck Loo. I didn't know what you had figured out. It was easier to just take you out of the picture."

I shook my head and chuckled a little.

"Boy, Sherman, I really wouldn't want to be in your shoes right now."

Fong glanced over at Frank.

"What's he talking about?"

Frank looked around. "I don't know," he said.

The quiet of the night was broken by a grinding metallic sound, as the door to the aircraft Quonset slid open on ancient, corroded bearings. Five men, all Asians, walked out.

They were all armed, a couple with sawed off Mossberg pump shotguns.

Frank was so stunned that he didn't bother stowing his weapon.

The men surrounded Frank and Sherman Fong.

"A trap, Eamon?" Frank said, finally realizing that his gun was a liability. He dropped it at his feet.

"I didn't expect it to be you," I said. "I'm sorry, Frank. I really am."

I slowly backed away, out of the spill of the mercury lamp.

A sixth man walked sadly out of the building, and into the deadly circle.

"I am ashamed," Sung said to Sherman Fong.

Fong glanced from Sung to each of the gunmen. He knew exactly what was going to happen, but he was helpless to do anything about it.

"You were wrong," he finally said to Sung. "What you were planning would have destroyed the peace in Chinatown. Don't you recall the Golden Dragon war?"

"It's a different place, now, Sherman," Sung said. "Since the Reds took over Hong Kong..."

"You are obsessed with the Communists!" Sherman yelled. "You don't see that they are being as poisoned by Hong Kong as they are poisoning it. It's only a matter of time before they collapse, just the way the Soviet Union did."

"As long as they don't control our business in Chinatown," Sung said. "I can wait. You know, though that the Communists have infiltrated at least one of the other tongs, maybe more. There is no other way."

"Um," I said, raising my hand. Sung turned to face me.

"Mr. Gold, you should leave now. At this moment, Mr. Fong and I are just having a conversation. Perhaps that is all you should know."

"Just a notion I had," I said. "If anything… violent were to happen to Fong, how would that affect the power structure among the tongs?"

"You already know the answer to that question," Sung said. "It doesn't matter which grass sandal falls. One is as good as another. Leave now. You don't want to be here."

"What about Inspector Raymond?" I asked.

"Leave *now*, Mr. Gold."

I took the ten hardest steps of my life, into the circle, to face Frank Raymond.

"My gun," I said.

"You're going to let them get away with this?" he said as I pulled the Browning from his pocket.

"You were ready to zag me here, tonight," I said. "How safe would I be, even if I had some way to save your skin? This is your play. You dealt this hand. I can't help you."

I holstered the Browning and started to walk away.

Then I stopped, and turned back to Sung Chow Li.

"He was my partner, once," I said, quietly. "I don't want him to…"

I looked back at Frank. He looked a hundred years old in the bleak, stark mercury vapor light.

"Just make it quick," I said.

TWENTY-TWO

As soon as I got back across the bridge, I ditched the Caddy in front of Louis Gai's office and took a cab over to Heidi's apartment. She was still asleep, but woke up the third time I rang the bell.

"Pack your bags," I told her, as I ushered her back into the apartment.

"What?"

"We have to get out of town, tonight."

She was still groggy, which probably made her more agreeable than usual.

"'kay," she said.

I used her computer to make quick reservations in Cancun, while she was packing. As soon as she was finished we cabbed over to my house, and I threw some things into an overnight case, just enough to get me through for a few days. The rest I could buy when we got where we were going.

From there, we took another cab to the airport. I paid cash for two roundtrip tickets on an AeroMexico flight to Cancun.

By first light, we were in the air over southern California, eating breakfast.

I couldn't explain what had happened while we were on the airplane, but later that day, on the beach at Isla de la Mujeres, I told her as much as I could.

"What's going to happen?" she asked.

"It's going to be bloody. Someone is sure to know that I helped set it off. It's better now to be far away."

"Can you go back?"

"When it's over. Until then, I guess I'm on vacation."

"One thing I don't understand," she said. "Sugar Wei. Where did she figure in?"

"I asked Sung the same thing when I met with him last night," I said. "He told me that Louis Gai sent her to me. She asked him for help when Buddy disappeared, and he knew about me from my association with Taylor Chu."

"That's it? It was just dumb luck?"

"Heidi, eighty percent of it is always just dumb luck."

––––––––

We stayed in Cancun for almost a month. The war lasted that long.

It made the Golden Dragon Massacre look like a schoolyard scuffle.

I missed the entire thing, but I read about it every day in the newspapers.

Two weeks after the trap in Alameda, Sung's limo was firebombed on Columbus. With him and Sherman Fong dead, the Sung Chow Li tong was decapitated, and that was the beginning of the end of the war.

In all, over two hundred members of the various tongs were killed in a little over three weeks. The Mayor called in the National Guard to keep the peace in Chinatown, and shortly after that the tong Dragon Heads had no choice but to talk things out, if they wanted to do any business at all.

Best of all, there was nobody left who knew the role I had played in the whole mess. On the day the newspapers announced an uneasy truce among the tongs, I made arrangements to go home.

We had been back in San Francisco for almost a month. Things were returning to normal, sort of. Heidi's gallery had begun to attract regular visitors again, and I had done a few skip traces for Doogie.

I was sitting in my office, munching on a plate of takeout fried clams and reading the Chronicle, when there was a knock on my door.

"Open," I called, as I folded the paper.

The door swung open, and Louis Gai walked in.

"Mr. Gai," I said, rising to my feet. I extended my hand.

"I'm happy to find you well, Mr. Gold," he said, as he took it.

"Please, have a seat."

He lowered himself into one of the leather-covered office chairs and surveyed me.

"What can I do for you?" I asked.

"I'll be brief. I have purchased Taylor Chu's law practice."

"Congratulations, I guess."

"Thank you. I have been examining his files, and it seems he used your services quite a bit more than I realized."

"Mr. Chu's retainer made up a big chunk of my yearly income."

"Yes, I could tell. Taylor spoke very highly of you. Before... before the recent troubles down in Chinatown, I sent a young woman to you."

"Wei Ma Lo. Her brother was missing."

"Yes. Very sad. You might like to know she has gone to work for me, in the new office."

"That's good news. I don't think her... uh, former career completely suited her."

"No. It's all temporary, of course. I've applied for her green card, and we're going to try to find a job for her where she can use her laboratory skills."

I nodded.

He seemed uncomfortable. After a moment, he shook his head.

"Well, then, I'm here to ask if you'd consider taking a retainer to handle the occasional investigation for me. The added workload of taking on Taylor's practice is stretching my usual investigators to the limit."

I did something really rude just then.

I swiveled my chair around and looked out my window toward the Golden Gate Bridge.

This would take some thought.

I knew a lot more about Gai now than I had when Taylor Chu was kidnapped. I knew he was tonged right up to the knot in his Givenchy tie. I suspected that, either because of Sherman Fong's manipulations or despite them, he was high on the list of potential grass sandals somewhere down in Chinatown. Working for him put me in high risk of stepping into something foul, early and often.

I swiveled the chair back to face him. I smiled, as sweetly and as benignly as I thought myself capable. "Sure, Louis. Let's talk."

ABOUT THE AUTHOR

Retired college professor and forensic psychologist Richard Helms has been nominated six times for the SMFS Derringer Award, winning it twice; five times for the Private Eye Writers of America Shamus Award; twice for the ITW Thriller Award, with one win; and once for the Mystery Readers International Macavity Award. He is also a frequent contributor to *Ellery Queen Mystery Magazine*, along with other periodicals. Mr. Helms is a former member of the Board of Directors of Mystery Writers of America, and the former president of the Southeast Regional Chapter of MWA. When not writing, Mr. Helms is an avid woodworker, and enjoys travel, gourmet cooking, and rooting for his beloved Carolina Tar Heels and Carolina Panthers. Richard Helms and his wife Elaine live in Charlotte, North Carolina.

Made in the USA
Middletown, DE
27 January 2019